Death in the Clouds

BY THE SAME AUTHOR

AGATHA CHRISTIE

DEATH IN
THE CLOUDS

HarperCollins*Publishers*

HarperCollins*Publishers*
77-85 Fulham Palace Road,
Hammersmith, London W6 8JB

This paperback edition 1994
3 5 7 9 8 6 4 2

Previously published in paperback by Fontana 1957
Reprinted twenty-two times

First published in Great Britain by
Collins 1935

Copyright Agatha Christie Mallowan 1935

ISBN 0 00 765948 2

Set in Plantin

Printed and bound in Great Britain by
Mackays of Chatham plc, Chatham, Kent

To Ormond Beadle

CONTENTS

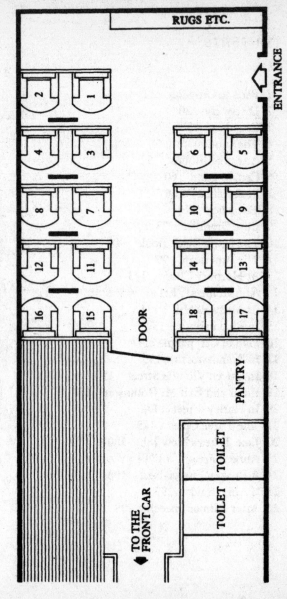

PASSENGERS

Seat

No. 2 MADAME GISELLE
No. 4 JAMES RYDER
No. 5 MONSIEUR ARMAND DUPONT
No. 6 MONSIEUR JEAN DUPONT
No. 8 DANIEL CLANCY
No. 9 HERCULE POIROT
No. 10 DOCTOR BRYANT
No. 12 NORMAN GALE
No. 13 THE COUNTESS OF HORBURY
No. 16 JANE GREY
No. 17 THE HON. VENETIA KERR

CHAPTER 1

Paris to Croydon

The September sun beat down hotly on Le Bourget aerodrome as the passengers crossed the ground and climbed into the air liner *Prometheus*, due to depart for Croydon in a few minutes' time.

Jane Grey was among the last to enter and take her seat, No. 16. Some of the passengers had already passed on through the centre door past the tiny pantry-kitchen and the two toilets to the front car. Most people were already seated. On the opposite side of the gangway there was a good deal of chatter – a rather shrill, high-pitched woman's voice dominating it. Jane's lips twisted slightly. She knew that particular type of voice so well.

'My dear – it's extraordinary – no idea – Where, do you say? Juan les Pins? Oh, yes. No – Le Pinet – Yes, just the same old crowd – But of *course* let's sit together. Oh, can't we? Who –? Oh, I see . . .'

And then a man's voice – foreign, polite:

'– With the greatest of pleasure, Madame.'

Jane stole a glance out of the corner of her eye.

A little elderly man with large moustaches and an egg-shaped head was politely moving himself and his belongings from the seat corresponding to Jane's on the opposite side of the gangway.

Jane turned her head slightly and got a view of the two women whose unexpected meeting had occasioned this polite action on the stranger's part. The mention of Le Pinet had stimulated her curiosity, for Jane also had been at Le Pinet.

She remembered one of the women perfectly – remembered how she had seen her last – at the baccarat table, her little hands clenching and unclenching themselves – her delicately made-up Dresden china face flushing and paling alternately. With a little effort, Jane thought, she could have remembered her name. A friend had mentioned it – had said: 'She's a peeress, she is, but not one of the proper ones – she was only some chorus girl or other.'

Deep scorn in the friend's voice. That had been Maisie, who had a first-class job as a masseuse 'taking off' flesh.

The other woman, Jane thought in passing, was the 'real thing'. The 'horsey, county type', thought Jane, and forthwith forgot the two women and interested herself in the view obtainable through the window of Le Bourget aerodrome. Various other machines were standing about. One of them looked like a big metallic centipede.

The one place she was obstinately determined not to look was straight in front of her, where, on the seat opposite, sat a young man.

He was wearing a rather bright periwinkle-blue pullover. Above the pullover Jane was determined not to look. If she did, she might catch his eye, and that would never do!

Mechanics shouted in French – the engine roared – relaxed – roared again – obstructions were pulled away – the plane started.

Jane caught her breath. It was only her second flight. She was still capable of being thrilled. It looked – it looked as though they must run into that fence thing – no, they were off the ground – rising – rising – sweeping round – there was Le Bourget beneath them.

The midday service to Croydon had started. It contained twenty-one passengers – ten in the forward carriage, eleven in the rear one. It had two pilots and two stewards. The noise of the engines was very skilfully deadened. There was no need to put cottonwool in the ears. Nevertheless there was enough noise to discourage conversation and encourage thought.

As the plane roared above France on its way to the

Channel the passengers in the rear compartment thought their various thoughts.

Jane Grey thought: 'I won't look at him . . . I won't . . . It's much better not. I'll go on looking out of the window and thinking. I'll choose a definite thing to think about – that's always the best way. That will keep my mind steady. I'll begin at the beginning and go all over it.'

Resolutely she switched her mind back to what she called the beginning, that purchase of a ticket in the Irish Sweep. It had been an extravagance, but an exciting extravagance.

A lot of laughter and teasing chatter in the hairdressing establishment in which Jane and five other young ladies were employed.

'What'll you do if you win it, dear?'

'I know what I'd do.'

Plans – castles in the air – a lot of chaff.

Well, she hadn't won 'it' – 'it' being the big prize; but she *had* won a hundred pounds.

A hundred pounds.

'You spend half of it, dear, and keep the other half for a rainy day. You never know.'

'I'd buy a fur coat, if I was you – a real tip-top one.'

'What about a cruise?'

Jane had wavered at the thought of a 'cruise', but in the end she had remained faithful to her first idea. A week at Le Pinet. So many of her ladies had been going to Le Pinet or just come back from Le Pinet. Jane, her clever fingers patting and manipulating the waves, her tongue uttering mechanically the usual clichés, 'Let me see, how long is it since you had your perm, Madam?' 'Your hair's such an uncommon colour, Madam.' 'What a wonderful summer it has been, hasn't it, Madam?' had thought to herself, 'Why the devil can't *I* go to Le Pinet?' Well, now she could.

Clothes presented small difficulty. Jane, like most

13

London girls employed in smart places, could produce a miraculous effect of fashion for a ridiculously small outlay. Nails, make-up and hair were beyond reproach.

Jane went to Le Pinet.

Was it possible that now, in her thoughts, ten days at Le Pinet had dwindled down to one incident?

An incident at the roulette table. Jane allowed herself a certain amount each evening for the pleasures of gambling. That sum she was determined not to exceed. Contrary to the prevalent superstition, Jane's beginner's luck had been bad. This was her fourth evening and the last stake of that evening. So far she had staked prudently on colour or on one of the dozens. She had won a little, but lost more. Now she waited, her stake in her hand.

There were two numbers on which nobody had staked, five and six. Should she put this, her last stake, on one of those numbers? If so, which of them? Five, or six? Which did she *feel*?

Five – five was going to turn up. The ball was spun. Jane stretched out her hand. Six, she'd put it on six.

Just in time. She and another player opposite staked simultaneously, she on six, he on five.

'*Rien ne va plus*,' said the croupier.

The ball clicked, settled.

'*Le numéro cinq, rouge, impair, manque.*'

Jane could have cried with vexation. The croupier swept away the stakes, paid out. The man opposite said: 'Aren't you going to take up your winnings?'

'Mine?'

'Yes.'

'But I put on six.'

'Indeed you didn't. I put on six and you put on five.'

He smiled – a very attractive smile. White teeth in a very brown face, blue eyes, crisp short hair.

Half unbelievingly Jane picked up her gains. Was it true? She felt a little muddled herself. Perhaps she *had* put her counters on five. She looked doubtingly at the stranger and he smiled easily back.

'That's right,' he said. 'Leave a thing lying there and somebody else will grab it who has got no right to it. That's an old trick.'

Then with a friendly little nod of the head he had moved away. That, too, had been nice of him. She might have suspected otherwise that he had let her take his winnings in order to scrape acquaintance with her. But he wasn't that kind of man. He was *nice* . . . (And here he was sitting opposite to her.)

And now it was all over – the money spent – a last two days (rather disappointing days) in Paris, and now home on her return air ticket.

'And what next?'

'Stop,' said Jane to her mind. 'Don't think of what's going to happen next. It'll only make you nervous.'

The two women had stopped talking.

She looked across the gangway. The Dresden china woman exclaimed petulantly, examining a broken fingernail. She rang the bell and when the white-coated steward appeared she said:

'Send my maid to me. She's in the other compartment.'

'Yes, my lady.'

The steward, very deferential, very quick and efficient, disappeared again. A dark-haired French girl dressed in black appeared. She carried a small jewel-case.

Lady Horbury spoke to her in French:

'Madeleine, I want my red morocco case.'

The maid passed along the gangway. At the extreme end of the car were some piled-up rugs and cases.

The girl returned with a small red dressing-case.

Cicely Horbury took it and dismissed the maid.

'That's all right, Madeleine. I'll keep it here.'

The maid went out again. Lady Horbury opened the case and from the beautifully fitted interior she extracted a nail

15

file. Then she looked long and earnestly at her face in a small mirror and touched it up here and there – a little powder, more lip salve.

Jane's lips curled scornfully; her glance travelled farther down the car.

Behind the two women was the little foreigner who had yielded his seat to the 'county' woman. Heavily muffled up in unnecessary mufflers, he appeared to be fast asleep. Perhaps made uneasy by Jane's scrutiny, his eyes opened, looked at her for a moment, then closed again.

Beside him sat a tall, grey-haired man with an authoritative face. He had a flute-case open in front of him and was polishing the flute with loving care. Funny, Jane thought, he didn't look like a musician – more like a lawyer or a doctor.

Behind those two were a couple of Frenchmen, one with a beard and one much younger – perhaps his son. They were talking and gesticulating in an excited manner.

On her own side of the car Jane's view was blocked by the man in the blue pullover, the man at whom, for some absurd reason, she was determined not to look.

'Absurd to feel – so – so excited. I might be seventeen,' thought Jane digustedly.

Opposite her, Norman Gale was thinking:

'She's pretty – really pretty . . . She remembers me all right. She looked so disappointed when her stakes were swept away. It was worth a lot more than that to see her pleasure when she won. I did that rather well . . . She's very attractive when she smiles – no pyorrhoea there – healthy gums and sound teeth . . . Damn it, I feel quite excited. Steady, my boy . . .'

He said to the steward who hovered at his side with the menu, 'I'll have cold tongue.'

The Countess of Horbury thought, 'My God, what shall I do? It's the hell of a mess – the hell of a mess. There's only one way out that I can see. If only I had the nerve. Can I do

16

it? Can I bluff it out? My nerves are all to pieces. That's the coke. Why did I ever take to coke? My face looks awful, simply awful. That cat Venetia Kerr being here makes it worse. She always looks at me as though I were dirt. Wanted Stephen herself. Well, she didn't get him! That long face of hers gets on my nerves. It's exactly like a horse. I hate these county women. My God, what shall I do? I've got to make up my mind. The old bitch meant what she said . . .'

She fumbled in her vanity bag for her cigarette-case and fitted a cigarette into a long holder. Her hands shook slightly.

The Honourable Venetia Kerr thought: 'Bloody little tart. That's what she is. She may be technically virtuous, but she's a tart through and through. Poor old Stephen . . . if he could only get rid of her . . .'

She in turn felt for her cigarette-case. She accepted Cicely Horbury's match.

The steward said, 'Excuse me, ladies, no smoking.'

Cicely Horbury said, 'Hell!'

M. Hercule Poirot thought, 'She is pretty, that little one over there. There is determination in that chin. Why is she so worried over something? Why is she so determined not to look at the handsome young man opposite her? She is very much aware of him and he of her . . .' The plane dropped slightly. '*Mon estomac*,' thought Hercule Poirot, and closed his eyes determinedly.

Beside him Dr Bryant, caressing his flute with nervous hands, thought, 'I can't decide. I simply cannot decide. This is the turning-point of my career . . .'

Nervously he drew out his flute from its case, caressingly, lovingly . . . Music . . . In music there was an escape from all your cares. Half smiling he raised the flute to his lips, then put it down again. The little man with the moustaches beside him was fast asleep. There had been a moment, when the plane had bumped a little, when he had

17

looked distinctly green. Dr Bryant was glad that he himself was neither train-sick nor sea-sick nor air-sick . . .

M. Dupont *père* turned excitedly in his seat and shouted at M. Dupont *fils* sitting beside him.

'There is no doubt about it. They are *all* wrong – the Germans, the Americans, the English! They date the pre-historic pottery all wrong. Take the Samarra ware –'

Jean Dupont, tall, fair, with a false air of indolence, said:

'You must take the evidences from all sources. There is Tall Halaf, and Sakje Geuze –'

They prolonged the discussion.

Armand Dupont wrenched open a battered attaché-case.

'Take these Kurdish pipes, such as they make today. The decoration on them is almost exactly similar to that on the pottery of 5000 BC.'

An eloquent gesture almost swept away the plate that a steward was placing in front of him.

Mr Clancy, writer of detective stories, rose from his seat behind Norman Gale and padded to the end of the car, extracted a continental Bradshaw from his raincoat pocket and returned with it to work out a complicated alibi for professional purposes.

Mr Ryder, in the seat behind him, thought, 'I'll have to keep my end up, but it's not going to be easy. I don't see how I'm going to raise the dibs for the next dividend . . . If we pass the dividend the fat's in the fire . . . Oh, hell!'

Norman Gale rose and went to the toilet. As soon as he had gone Jane drew out a mirror and surveyed her face anxiously. She also applied powder and lipstick.

A steward placed coffee in front of her.

Jane looked out of the window. The Channel showed blue and shining below.

A wasp buzzed round Mr Clancy's head just as he was dealing with 19.55 at Tzaribrod, and he struck at it absently. The wasp flew off to investigate the Duponts' coffee cups.

Jean Dupont slew it neatly.

Peace settled down on the car. Conversation ceased, but thoughts pursued their way.

Right at the end of the car, in seat No. 2, Madame Giselle's head lolled forward a little. One might have taken her to be asleep. But she was not asleep. She neither spoke nor thought.

Madame Giselle was dead . . .

CHAPTER 2

Discovery

Henry Mitchell, the senior of the two stewards, passed swiftly from table to table depositing bills. In half an hour's time they would be at Croydon. He gathered up notes and silver, bowed, said, 'Thank you, sir. Thank you, Madam.' At the table where the two Frenchmen sat he had to wait a minute or two, they were so busy discussing and gesticulating. And there wouldn't be much of a tip anyway from them, he thought gloomily. Two of the passengers were asleep – the little man with the moustaches, and the old woman down at the end. She was a good tipper, though – he remembered her crossing several times. He refrained therefore from awaking her.

The little man with the moustaches woke up and paid for the bottle of soda water and the thin captain biscuits, which was all he had had.

Mitchell left the other passenger as long as possible. About five minutes before they reached Croydon he stood by her side and leant over her.

'Pardon, Madam, your bill.'

He laid a deferential hand on her shoulder. She did not wake. He increased the pressure, shaking her gently, but the only result was an unexpected slumping of the body down in the seat. Mitchell bent over her, then straightened up with a white face.

Albert Davis, second steward, said:

'Coo! You don't mean it!'

'I tell you it's true.'

Mitchell was white and shaking.

'You *sure*, Henry?'

'Dead sure. At least – well, I suppose it might be a fit.'

'We'll be at Croydon in a few minutes.'

'If she's just taken bad –'

They remained a minute or two undecided – then arranged their course of action. Mitchell returned to the rear car. He went from table to table, bending his head and murmuring confidentially:

'Excuse me, sir, you don't happen to be a doctor –?'

Norman Gale said, 'I'm a dentist. But if there's anything I can do –?' He half rose from his seat.

'I'm a doctor,' said Dr Bryant. 'What's the matter?'

'There's a lady at the end there – I don't like the look of her.'

Bryant rose to his feet and accompanied the steward. Unnoticed, the little man with the moustaches followed them.

Dr Bryant bent over the huddled figure in seat No. 2, the figure of a stoutish middle-aged woman dressed in heavy black.

The doctor's examination was brief.

He said: 'She's dead.'

Mitchell said, 'What do you think it was – kind of fit?'

'That I can't possibly say without a detailed examination. When did you last see her – alive, I mean?'

Mitchell reflected.

'She was all right when I brought her coffee along.'

'When was that?'

'Well, it might have been three-quarters of an hour ago – about that. Then, when I brought the bill along, I thought she was asleep . . .'

Bryant said, 'She's been dead at least half an hour.'

Their consultation was beginning to cause interest – heads were craned round looking at them. Necks were stretched to listen.

'I suppose it might have been a kind of fit, like?' suggested Mitchell hopefully.

21

He clung to the theory of a fit.

His wife's sister had fits. He felt that fits were homely things that any man might understand.

Dr Bryant had no intention of committing himself. He merely shook his head with a puzzled expression.

A voice spoke at his elbow, the voice of the muffled-up man with the moustaches.

'There is,' he said, 'a mark on her neck.'

He spoke apologetically, with a due sense of speaking to superior knowledge.

'True,' said Dr Bryant.

The woman's head lolled over sideways. There was a minute puncture mark on the side of her throat.

'Pardon –' the two Duponts joined in. They had been listening for the last few minutes. 'The lady is dead, you say, and there is a mark on the neck?'

It was Jean, the younger Dupont, who spoke.

'May I make a suggestion? There was a wasp flying about. I killed it.' He exhibited the corpse in his coffee saucer. 'Is it not possible that the poor lady has died of a wasp sting? I have heard such things happen.'

'It is possible,' agreed Bryant. 'I have known of such cases. Yes, that is certainly quite a possible explanation, especially if there were any cardiac weakness –'

'Anything I'd better do, sir?' asked the steward. 'We'll be at Croydon in a minute.'

'Quite, quite,' said Dr Bryant as he moved away a little. 'There's nothing to be done. The – er – body must not be moved, steward.'

'Yes, sir, I quite understand.'

Dr Bryant prepared to resume his seat and looked in some surprise at the small muffled-up foreigner who was standing his ground.

'My dear sir,' he said, 'the best thing to do is to go back to your seat. We shall be at Croydon almost immediately.'

'That's right, sir,' said the steward. He raised his voice.

'Please resume your seats, everybody.'

'*Pardon*,' said the little man. 'There is something –'

'Something?'

'*Mais oui*, something that has been overlooked.'

With the tip of a pointed patent-leather shoe he made his meaning clear. The steward and Dr Bryant followed the action with their eyes. They caught the glint of yellow and black on the floor half concealed by the edge of the black skirt.

'Another wasp?' said the doctor, surprised.

Hercule Poirot went down on his knees. He took a small pair of tweezers from his pocket and used them delicately. He stood up with his prize.

'Yes,' he said, 'it is very like a wasp; but it is not a wasp!'

He turned the object about this way and that so that both the doctor and the steward could see it clearly, a little knot of teased fluffy silk, orange and black, attached to a long, peculiar-looking thorn with a discoloured tip.

'Good gracious! Good gracious me!' The exclamation came from little Mr Clancy, who had left his seat and was poking his head desperately over the steward's shoulder. 'Remarkable, really very remarkable, absolutely the most remarkable thing I have ever come across in my life. Well, upon my soul, I should never have believed it.'

'Could you make yourself just a little clearer, sir?' asked the steward. 'Do you recognize this?'

'Recognize it? Certainly I recognize it.' Mr Clancy swelled with passionate pride and gratification. 'This object, gentlemen, is the native thorn shot from a blowpipe by certain tribes – er – I cannot be exactly certain now if it is South American tribes or whether it is the inhabitants of Borneo which I have in mind; but that is undoubtedly a native dart that has been aimed by a blowpipe, and I strongly suspect that on the tip –'

'Is the famous arrow poison of the South American

23

Indians,' finished Hercule Poirot. And he added, '*Mais enfin! Est-ce que c'est possible?*'

'It is certainly very extraordinary,' said Mr Clancy, still full of blissful excitement. 'As I say most extraordinary. I am myself a writer of detective fiction; but actually to meet, in real life –'

Words failed him.

The aeroplane heeled slowly over, and those people who were standing up staggered a little. The plane was circling round in its descent to Croydon aerodrome.

CHAPTER 3

Croydon

The steward and the doctor were no longer in charge of the situation. Their place was usurped by the rather absurd-looking little man in the mufflers. He spoke with an authority and a certainty of being obeyed that no one thought of questioning.

He whispered to Mitchell, and the latter nodded, and, pushing his way through the passengers, he took up his stand in the doorway leading past the toilets to the front car.

The plane was running along the ground now. When it finally came to a stop Mitchell raised his voice:

'I must ask you, ladies and gentlemen, to keep your seats and remain here until somebody in authority takes charge. I hope you will not be detained long.'

The reasonableness of this order was appreciated by most of the occupants of the car, but one person protested shrilly.

'Nonsense,' cried Lady Horbury angrily. 'Don't you know who I am? I insist on being allowed to leave at once.'

'Very sorry, my lady. Can't make exceptions.'

'But it's absurd, absolutely absurd,' Cicely tapped her foot angrily. 'I shall report you to the company. It's outrageous that we should be shut up here with a dead body.'

'Really, my dear,' Venetia Kerr spoke with her well-bred drawl, 'too devastating, but I fancy we'll have to put up with it.' She herself sat down and drew out a cigarette-case. 'Can I smoke now, steward?'

The harassed Mitchell said, 'I don't suppose it matters now, Miss.'

He glanced over his shoulder. Davis had disembarked the passengers from the front car by the emergency door and had now gone in search of orders.

25

The wait was not a long one, but it seemed to the passengers as though half an hour at least had passed before an erect soldierly figure in plain clothes, accompanied by a uniformed policeman, came hurriedly across the aerodrome and climbed into the plane by the door that Mitchell held open.

'Now, then, what's all this?' demanded the new-comer in brisk official tones.

He listened to Mitchell and then to Dr Bryant, and he flung a quick glance over the crumpled figure of the dead woman.

He gave an order to the constable and then addressed the passengers.

'Will you please follow me, ladies and gentlemen?'

He escorted them out of the plane and across the aerodrome, but he did not enter the usual customs department; instead, he brought them to a small private room.

'I hope not to keep you waiting any longer than is unavoidable, ladies and gentlemen.'

'Look here, Inspector,' said Mr James Ryder. 'I have an important business engagement in London.'

'Sorry, sir.'

'I am Lady Horbury. I consider it absolutely outrageous that I should be detained in this matter!'

'I'm sincerely sorry, Lady Horbury; but, you see, this is a very serious matter. It looks like a case of murder.'

'The arrow poison of the South American Indians,' murmured Mr Clancy deliriously, a happy smile on his face.

The inspector looked at him suspiciously.

The French archaeologist spoke excitedly in French, and the inspector replied to him slowly and carefully in the same language.

Venetia Kerr said, 'All this is a most crashing bore, but I suppose you have your duty to do, Inspector,' to which that worthy replied, 'Thank you, Madam,' in accents of some gratitude.

He went on:

'If you ladies and gentlemen will remain here, I want a few words with Doctor – er – Doctor –?'

'Bryant, my name is.'

'Thank you. Just come this way with me, Doctor.'

'May I assist at your interview?'

It was the little man with the moustaches who spoke.

The inspector turned on him, a sharp retort on his lips. Then his face changed suddenly.

'Sorry, M. Poirot,' he said. 'You're so muffled up, I didn't recognize you. Come along, by all means.'

He held the door open and Bryant and Poirot passed through, followed by the suspicious glance of the rest of the company.

'And why should he be allowed out and we made to stay here?' cried Cicely Horbury.

Venetia Kerr sat down resignedly on a bench.

'Probably one of the French police,' she said, 'or a customs spy.'

She lit a cigarette.

Norman Gale said rather diffidently to Jane:

'I think I saw you at – er – Le Pinet.'

'I was at Le Pinet.'

Norman Gale said, 'It's an awfully attractive place. I like the pine trees.'

Jane said, 'Yes, they smell so nice.'

And then they both paused for a minute or two, uncertain what to say next.

Finally Gale said, 'I – er – recognized you at once in the plane.'

Jane expressed great surprise. 'Did you?'

Gale said, 'Do you think that woman was really murdered?'

'I suppose so,' said Jane. 'It's rather thrilling in a way, but it's rather nasty too,' and she shuddered a little, and Norman Gale moved just a little nearer in a protective manner.

The Duponts were talking French to each other. Mr Ryder was making calculations in a little notebook and looking at his watch from time to time. Cicely Horbury sat with her foot tapping impatiently on the floor. She lit a cigarette with a shaking hand.

Against the door on the inside leaned a very large blue-clad impassive-looking policeman.

In a room nearby Inspector Japp was talking to Dr Bryant and Hercule Poirot.

'You've got a knack of turning up in the most unexpected places, M. Poirot.'

'Isn't Croydon aerodrome a little out of your beat, my friend?' asked Poirot.

'Ah, I'm after rather a big bug in the smuggling line. A bit of luck my being on the spot. This is the most amazing business I've come across for years. Now, then, let's get down to it. First of all, Doctor, perhaps you'll give me your full name and address.'

'Roger James Bryant. I am a specialist on diseases of the ear and throat. My address is 329 Harley Street.'

A stolid constable sitting at a table took down these particulars.

'Our own surgeon will, of course, examine the body,' said Japp, 'but we shall want you at the inquest, Doctor.'

'Quite so, quite so.'

'Can you give us any idea of the time of death?'

'The woman must have been dead at least half an hour when I examined her; that was a few minutes before we arrived at Croydon. I can't go nearer than that, but I understand from the steward that he had spoken to her about an hour before.'

'Well, that narrows it down for all practical purposes. I suppose it's no good asking you if you observed anything of a suspicious nature?'

The doctor shook his head.

'And me, I was asleep,' said Poirot with deep chagrin. 'I

suffer almost as badly in the air as on the sea. Always I wrap myself up well and try to sleep.'

'Any idea as to the cause of death, Doctor?'

'I should not like to say anything definite at this stage. This is a case for post-mortem examination and analysis.'

Japp nodded comprehendingly.

'Well, Doctor,' he said, 'I don't think we need detain you now. I'm afraid you'll – er – have to go through certain formalities; all the passengers will. We can't make exceptions.'

Dr Bryant smiled.

'I should prefer you to make sure that I have no – er – blowpipes or other lethal weapons concealed upon my person,' he said gravely.

'Rogers here will see to that.' Japp nodded to his subordinate. 'By the way, Doctor, have you any idea what would be likely to be on this –?'

He indicated the discoloured thorn which was lying in a small box on the table in front of him.

Dr Bryant shook his head.

'Difficult to say without an analysis. Curare is the usual poison employed by the natives, I believe.'

'Would that do the trick?'

'It is a very swift and rapid poison.'

'But not very easy to obtain, eh?'

'Not at all easy for a layman.'

'Then we'll have to search you extra carefully,' said Japp, who was always fond of his joke. 'Rogers!'

The doctor and the constable left the room together.

Japp tilted back his chair and looked at Poirot.

'Rum business, this,' he said. 'Bit too sensational to be true. I mean, blowpipes and poisoned darts in an aeroplane – well, it insults one's intelligence.'

'That, my friend, is a very profound remark,' said Poirot.

'A couple of my men are searching the plane,' said Japp.

'We've got a fingerprint man and a photographer coming along. I think we'd better see the stewards next.'

He strode to the door and gave an order. The two stewards were ushered in. The younger steward had recovered his balance. He looked more excited than anything else. The other steward still looked white and frightened.

'That's all right, my lads,' said Japp. 'Sit down. Got the passports there? Good.'

He sorted through them quickly.

'Ah, here we are. Marie Morisot – French passport. Know anything about her?'

'I've seen her before. She crossed to and fro from England fairly often,' said Mitchell.

'Ah! in business of some kind. You don't know what her business was?'

Mitchell shook his head. The younger steward said, 'I remember her too. I saw her on the early service – the eight o'clock from Paris.'

'Which of you was the last to see her alive?'

'Him.' The younger steward indicated his companion.

'That's right,' said Mitchell. 'That's when I took her her coffee.'

'How was she looking then?'

'Can't say I noticed. I just handed her the sugar and offered her milk, which she refused.'

'What time was that?'

'Well, I couldn't say exactly. We were over the Channel at the time. Might have been somewhere about two o'clock.'

'Thereabouts,' said Albert Davis, the other steward.

'When did you see her next?'

'When I took the bills round.'

'What time was that?'

'About a quarter of an hour later. I thought she was asleep – Crikey, she must have been dead then!'

The steward's voice sounded awed.

'You didn't see any signs of this –' Japp indicated the little wasp-like dart.

'No, sir, I didn't.'

'What about you, Davis?'

'The last time I saw her was when I was handing the biscuits to go with the cheese. She was all right then.'

'What is your system of serving meals?' asked Poirot. 'Do each of you serve separate cars?'

'No, sir, we work it together. The soup, then the meat and vegetables and salad, then the sweet, and so on. We usually serve the rear car first, and then go out with a fresh lot of dishes to the front car.'

Poirot nodded.

'Did this Morisot woman speak to anyone on the plane, or show any signs of recognition?' asked Japp.

'Not that I saw, sir.'

'You, Davis?'

'No, sir.'

'Did she leave her seat at all during the journey?'

'I don't think so, sir.'

'There's nothing you can think of that throws any light on this business – either of you?'

Both the men thought, then shook their heads.

'Well, that will be all for now, then. I'll see you again later.'

Henry Mitchell said soberly:

'It's a nasty thing to happen, sir. I don't like it, me having been in charge, so to speak.'

'Well, I can't see that you're to blame in any way,' said Japp. 'Still, I agree, it's a nasty thing to happen.'

He made a gesture of dismissal. Poirot leaned forward.

'Permit me one little question.'

'Go ahead, M. Poirot.'

'Did either of you two notice a wasp flying about the plane?'

Both men shook their heads.

'There was no wasp that I know of,' said Mitchell.

'There *was* a wasp,' said Poirot. 'We have its dead body on the plate of one of the passengers.'

'Well, I didn't see it, sir,' said Mitchell.

'No more did I,' said Davis.

'No matter.'

The two stewards left the room. Japp was running his eye rapidly over the passports.

'Got a countess on board,' he said. 'She's the one who's throwing her weight about, I suppose. Better see her first before she goes right off the handle and gets a question asked in the House about the brutal methods of the police.'

'You will, I suppose, search very carefully all the baggage – the hand baggage – of the passengers in the rear car of the plane?'

Japp winked cheerfully.

'Why, what do you think, M. Poirot? We've got to find that blowpipe – if there *is* a blowpipe and we're not all dreaming! Seems like a kind of nightmare to me. I suppose that little writer chap hasn't gone off his onion and decided to do one of his crimes in the flesh instead of on paper? This poisoned dart business sounds like him.'

Poirot shook his head doubtfully.

'Yes,' continued Japp, 'everybody's got to be searched, whether they kick up rough or not; and every bit of truck they had with them has got to be searched too – and that's flat.'

'A very exact list might be made, perhaps,' suggested Poirot, 'a list of everything in these people's possession.'

Japp looked at him curiously.

'That can be done if you say so, M. Poirot. I don't quite see what you're driving at, though. We know what we're looking for.'

'*You* may, perhaps, *mon ami*, but *I* am not so sure. I look for something, but I know not what it is.'

'At it again, M. Poirot! You do like making things

difficult, don't you? Now for her ladyship before she's quite ready to scratch my eyes out.'

Lady Horbury, however, was noticeably calmer in her manner. She accepted a chair and answered Japp's questions without the least hesitation. She described herself as the wife of the Earl of Horbury, gave her address as Horbury Chase, Sussex, and 315 Grosvenor Square, London. She was returning to London from Le Pinet and Paris. The deceased woman was quite unknown to her. She had noticed nothing suspicious during the flight over. In any case, she was facing the other way – towards the front of the plane – so had had no opportunity of seeing anything that was going on behind her. She had not left her seat during the journey. As far as she remembered no one had entered the rear car from the front one with the exception of the stewards. She could not remember exactly, but she thought that two of the men passengers had left the rear car to go to the toilets, but she was not sure of this. She had not observed anyone handling anything that could be likened to a blowpipe. No – in answer to Poirot – she had not noticed a wasp in the car.

Lady Horbury was dismissed. She was succeeded by the Honourable Venetia Kerr.

Miss Kerr's evidence was much the same as that of her friend. She gave her name as Venetia Anne Kerr, and her address as Little Paddocks, Horbury, Sussex. She herself was returning from the South of France. As far as she was aware she had never seen the deceased before. She had noticed nothing suspicious during the journey. Yes, she had seen some of the passengers farther down the car striking at a wasp. One of them, she thought, had killed it. That was after luncheon had been served.

Exit Miss Kerr.

'You seem very much interested in that wasp, M. Poirot.'

'The wasp is not so much interesting as suggestive, eh?'

'If you ask me,' said Japp, changing the subject, 'those

33

two Frenchmen are the ones in this! They were just across the gangway from the Morisot woman. They're a seedy-looking couple, and that battered old suitcase of theirs is fairly plastered with outlandish foreign labels. Shouldn't be surprised if they'd been to Borneo or South America, or wherever it is. Of course, we can't get a line on the motive, but I dare say we can get that from Paris. We'll have to get the Sûreté to collaborate over this. It's their job more than ours. But, if you ask me, those two toughs are our meat.'

Poirot's eyes twinkled a little.

'What you say is possible, certainly, but as regards some of your points you are in error, my friend. Those two men are not toughs – or cut-throats, as you suggest. They are on the contrary two very distinguished and learned archaeologists.'

'Go on – you're pulling my leg!'

'Not at all. I know them by sight perfectly. They are M. Armand Dupont and his son, M. Jean Dupont. They have returned not long ago from conducting some very interesting excavations in Persia at a site not far from Susa.'

'Go on!'

Japp made a grab at a passport.

'You're right, M. Poirot,' he said, 'but you must admit they don't look up to much, do they?'

'The world's famous men seldom do! I myself – *moi, qui vous parle* – I have before now been taken for a hairdresser!'

'You don't say so,' said Japp with a grin. 'Well, let's have a look at our distinguished archaeologists.'

M. Dupont *père* declared that the deceased was quite unknown to him. He had noticed nothing of what had happened on the journey over as he had been discussing a very interesting point with his son. He had not left his seat at all. Yes, he had noticed a wasp towards the end of lunch. His son had killed it.

M. Jean Dupont confirmed this evidence. He had noticed nothing of what went on round about him. The wasp had annoyed him and he had killed it. What had been the subject of the discussion? The prehistoric pottery of the Near East.

Mr Clancy, who came next, came in for rather a bad time. Mr Clancy, so felt Inspector Japp, knew altogether too much about blowpipes and poisoned darts.

'Have you ever owned a blowpipe yourself?'

'Well – I – er – well, yes, as a matter of fact I have.'

'Indeed!' Inspector Japp pounced on the statement.

Little Mr Clancy fairly squeaked with agitation.

'You must not – er – misunderstand; my motives are quite innocent. I can explain . . .'

'Yes, sir, perhaps you *will* explain.'

'Well, you see, I was writing a book in which the murder was committed that way –'

'Indeed –'

Again that threatening intonation. Mr Clancy hurried on:

'It was all a question of fingerprints – if you understand me. It was necessary to have an illustration illustrating the point I meant – I mean – the fingerprints – the position of them – the position of them on the blowpipe, if you understand me, and having noticed such a thing – in the Charing Cross Road it was – at least two years ago now – and so I bought the blowpipe – and an artist friend of mine very kindly drew it for me – with the fingerprints – to illustrate my point. I can refer you to the book – *The Clue of the Scarlet Petal* – and my friend too.'

'Did you keep the blowpipe?'

'Why, yes – why, yes, I think so – I mean, yes, I did.'

'And where is it now?'

'Well, I suppose – well, it must be somewhere about.'

'What exactly do you mean by somewhere about, Mr Clancy?'

'I mean – well – somewhere – I can't say where. I – I am not a very tidy man.'

'It isn't with you now, for instance?'

35

'Certainly not. Why, I haven't see the thing for nearly six months.'

Inspector Japp bent a glance of cold suspicion on him and continued his questions.

'Did you leave your seat at all in the plane?'

'No, certainly not – at least – well, yes, I did.'

'Oh, you *did*. Where did you go?'

'I went to get a continental Bradshaw out of my raincoat pocket. The raincoat was piled with some rugs and suitcases by the entrance at the end.'

'So you passed close by the deceased's seat?'

'No – at least – well, yes, I must have done. But this was long before anything could have happened. I'd only just drunk my soup.'

Further questions drew negative answers. Mr Clancy had noticed nothing suspicious. He had been absorbed in the perfectioning of his cross-Europe alibi.

'Alibi, eh?' said the inspector darkly.

Poirot intervened with a question about wasps.

Yes, Mr Clancy had noticed a wasp. It had attacked him. He was afraid of wasps. When was this? Just after the steward had brought him his coffee. He struck at it and it went away.

Mr Clancy's name and address were taken and he was allowed to depart, which he did with relief on his face.

'Looks a bit fishy to me,' said Japp. 'He actually *had* a blowpipe; and look at his manner. All to pieces.'

'That is the severity of your official demeanour, my good Japp.'

'There's nothing for anyone to be afraid of if they're only telling the truth,' said the Scotland Yard man austerely.

Poirot looked at him pityingly.

'In verity, I believe that you yourself honestly believe that.'

'Of course I do. It's true. Now, then, let's have Norman Gale.'

Norman Gale gave his address as 14 Shepherd's Avenue, Muswell Hill. By profession he was a dentist. He was returning from a holiday spent at Le Pinet on the French coast. He had spent a day in Paris looking at various new types of dental instruments.

He had never seen the deceased, and had noticed nothing suspicious during the journey. In any case, he had been facing the other way – towards the front car. He had left his seat once during the journey to go to the toilet. He had returned straight to his seat and had never been near the rear end of the car. He had not noticed any wasp.

After him came James Ryder, somewhat on edge and brusque in manner. He was returning from a business visit to Paris. He did not know the deceased. Yes, he had occupied the seat immediately in front of hers, but he could not have seen her without rising and looking over the back of his seat. He had heard nothing – no cry or exclamation. No one had come down the car except the stewards. Yes, the two Frenchmen had occupied the seats across the gangway from his. They had talked practically the whole journey. The younger of the two had killed a wasp at the conclusion of the meal. No, he hadn't noticed the wasp previously. He didn't know what a blowpipe was like, as he'd never seen one, so he couldn't say if he'd seen one on the journey or not –

Just at this point there was a tap on the door. A police constable entered, subdued triumph in his bearing.

'The sergeant's just found this, sir,' he said. 'Thought you'd like to have it at once.'

He laid his prize on the table, unwrapping it with care from the handkerchief in which it was folded.

'No fingerprints, sir, so as the sergeant can see, but he told me to be careful.'

The object thus displayed was an undoubted blowpipe of native manufacture.

Japp drew his breath in sharply.

'Good Lord! Then it *is* true? Upon my soul, I didn't believe it!'

Mr Ryder leant forward interestedly.

'So that's what the South Americans use, is it? Read about such things, but never seen one. Well, I can answer your question now. I didn't see anyone handling anything of this type.'

'Where was it found?' asked Japp sharply.

'Pushed down out of sight behind one of the seats, sir.'

'Which seat?'

'No. 9.'

'Very entertaining,' said Poirot.

Japp turned to him.

'What's entertaining about it?'

'Only that No. 9 was *my* seat.'

'Well, that looks a bit odd for you, I must say,' said Mr Ryder.

Japp frowned.

'Thank you, Mr Ryder, that will do.'

When Ryder had gone he turned to Poirot with a grin.

'This *your* work, old bird?'

'*Mon ami*,' said Poirot with dignity, 'when I commit a murder it will *not* be with the arrow poison of the South American Indians.'

'It *is* a bit low,' agreed Japp. 'But it seems to have worked.'

'That is what gives one so furiously to think.'

'Whoever it was must have taken the most stupendous chances. Yes, by Jove, they must. Lord, the fellow must have been an absolute lunatic. Who have we got left? Only one girl. Let's have her in and get it over. Jane Grey – sounds like a history book.'

'She is a pretty girl,' said Poirot.

'Is she, you old dog? So you weren't asleep all the time, eh?'

'She was pretty – and nervous,' said Poirot.

'Nervous, eh?' said Japp alertly.

'Oh, my dear friend, when a girl is nervous it usually means a young man – not crime.'

'Oh, well, I suppose you're right. Here she is.'

Jane answered the questions put to her clearly enough. Her name was Jane Grey and she was employed at Messrs. Antoine's hairdressing establishment in Bruton Street. Her home address was 10 Harrogate Street, NW5. She was returning to England from Le Pinet.

'Le Pinet – h'm!'

Further questions drew the story of the Sweep ticket.

'Ought to be made illegal, those Irish Sweeps,' growled Japp.

'I think they're marvellous,' said Jane. 'Haven't *you* ever put half a crown on a horse?'

Japp blushed and looked confused.

The questions were resumed. Shown the blowpipe, Jane denied having seen it at any time. She did not know the deceased, but had noticed her at Le Bourget.

'What made you notice her particularly?'

'Because she was so frightfully ugly,' said Jane truthfully.

Nothing else of any value was elicited from her, and she was allowed to go.

Japp fell back into contemplation of the blowpipe.

'It beats me,' he said. 'The crudest detective story dodge coming out trumps! What have we got to look for now? A man who's travelled in the part of the world this thing comes from? And where exactly does it come from? Have to get an expert on to that. It may be Malayan or South American or African.'

'Originally, yes,' said Poirot. 'But if you observe closely, my friend, you will notice a microscopic piece of paper adhering to the pipe. It looks to me very much like the remains of a torn-off price ticket. I fancy that this particular specimen has journeyed from the wilds *via* some curio

39

dealer's shop. That will possibly make our search more easy. Just one little question.'

'Ask away.'

'You will still have that list made – the list of the passengers' belongings?'

'Well, it isn't quite so vital now, but it might as well be done. You're very set on that?'

'*Mais oui*. I am puzzled, very puzzled. If I could find something to help me –'

Japp was not listening. He was examining the torn price ticket.

'Clancy let out that he bought a blowpipe. These detective-story writers . . . always making the police out to be fools . . . and getting their procedure all wrong. Why, if I were to say the things to my super that their inspectors say to superintendents I should be thrown out of the Force tomorrow on my ear. Set of ignorant scribblers! This is just the sort of damn-fool murder that a scribbler of rubbish would think he could get away with.'

CHAPTER 4

The Inquest

The inquest on Marie Morisot was held four days later. The sensational manner of her death had aroused great public interest, and the coroner's court was crowded.

The first witness called was a tall elderly Frenchman with a grey beard – Maître Alexandre Thibault. He spoke English slowly and precisely with a slight accent, but quite idiomatically.

After the preliminary questions the coroner asked, 'You have viewed the body of the deceased. Do you recognize it?'

'I do. It is that of my client, Marie Angélique Morisot.'

'That is the name on the deceased's passport. Was she known to the public by another name?'

'Yes, that of Madame Giselle.'

A stir of excitement went around. Reporters sat with pencils poised. The coroner said, 'Will you tell us exactly who this Madame Morisot – or Madame Giselle – was?'

'Madame Giselle – to give her her professional name, the name under which she did business – was one of the best-known moneylenders in Paris.'

'She carried on her business – where?'

'At the Rue Joliette, No. 3. That was also her private residence.'

'I understand that she journeyed to England fairly frequently. Did her business extend to this country?'

'Yes. Many of her clients were English people. She was very well known amongst a certain section of English society.'

'How would you describe that section of society?'

'Her clientèle was mostly among the upper and professional classes, in cases where it was important that the utmost discretion should be observed.'

'She had the reputation of being discreet?'

'Extremely discreet.'

'May I ask if you have an intimate knowledge of – er – her various business transactions?'

'No. I dealt with her legal business, but Madame Giselle was a first-class woman of business, thoroughly capable of attending to her own affairs in the most competent manner. She kept the control of her business entirely in her own hands. She was, if I may say so, a woman of very original character, and a well-known public figure.'

'To the best of your knowledge, was she a rich woman at the time of her death?'

'She was an extremely wealthy woman.'

'Had she, to your knowledge, any enemies?'

'Not to my knowledge.'

Maître Thibault then stepped down and Henry Mitchell was called.

The coroner said, 'Your name is Henry Charles Mitchell and you reside at 11 Shoeblack Lane, Wandsworth?'

'Yes, sir.'

'You are in the employment of Universal Airlines, Ltd?'

'Yes, sir.'

'You are the senior steward on the air liner *Prometheus*?'

'Yes, sir.'

'On Tuesday last, the eighteenth, you were on duty on the *Prometheus* on the twelve o'clock service from Paris to Croydon. The deceased travelled by that service. Had you ever seen the deceased before?'

'Yes, sir. I was on the 8.45 am service six months ago and I noticed her travelling by that once or twice.'

'Did you know her name?'

'Well, it must have been on my list, sir, but I didn't notice it special, so to speak.'

'Have you ever heard the name of Madame Giselle?'

'No, sir.'

'Please describe the occurrences of Tuesday last in your own way.'

42

'I'd served the luncheons, sir, and was coming round with the bills. The deceased was, as I thought, asleep. I decided not to wake her until about five minutes before we got in. When I tried to do so I discovered that she was dead or seriously ill. I discovered that there was a doctor on board. He said –'

'We shall have Dr Bryant's evidence presently. Will you take a look at this?'

The blowpipe was handed to Mitchell, who took it gingerly.

'Have you ever seen that before?'

'No, sir.'

'You are certain that you did not see it in the hands of any of the passengers?'

'Yes, sir.'

'Albert Davis.'

The younger steward took the stand.

'You are Albert Davis of 23 Barcome Street, Croydon. You are employed by Universal Airlines, Ltd?'

'Yes, sir.'

'You were on duty on the *Prometheus* as second steward on Tuesday last?'

'Yes, sir.'

'What was the first that you knew of the tragedy?'

'Mr Mitchell, sir, told me that he was afraid something had happened to one of the passengers.'

'Have you ever seen this before?'

The blowpipe was handed to Davis.

'No, sir.'

'You did not observe it in the hands of any of the passengers?'

'No, sir.'

'Did anything at all happen on the journey that you think might throw light on this affair?'

'No, sir.'

'Very good. You may stand down.'

'Dr Roger Bryant.'

Dr Bryant gave his name and address and described himself as a specialist in ear and throat diseases.

'Will you tell us in your own words, Dr Bryant, exactly what happened on Tuesday last, the eighteenth?'

'Just before getting into Croydon I was approached by the chief steward. He asked me if I was a doctor. On my replying in the affirmative, he told me that one of the passengers had been taken ill. I rose and went with him. The woman in question was lying slumped down in her seat. She had been dead some time.'

'What length of time in your opinion, Dr Bryant?'

'I should say at least half an hour. Between half an hour and an hour would be my estimate.'

'Did you form any theory as to the cause of death?'

'No. It would have been impossible to say without a detailed examination.'

'But you noticed a small puncture on the side of the neck?'

'Yes.'

'Thank you . . . Dr James Whistler.'

Dr Whistler was a thin, scraggy little man.

'You are the police surgeon for this district?'

'I am.'

'Will you give your evidence in your own words?'

'Shortly after three o'clock on Tuesday last, the eighteenth, I received a summons to Croydon aerodrome. There I was shown the body of a middle-aged woman in one of the seats of the air liner *Prometheus*. She was dead, and death had occurred, I should say, about an hour previously. I noticed a circular puncture on the side of the neck – directly on the jugular vein. This mark was quite consistent with having been caused by the sting of a wasp or by the insertion of a thorn which was shown to me. The body was removed to the mortuary, where I was able to make a detailed examination.'

'What conclusions did you come to?'

'I came to the conclusion that death was caused by the introduction of a powerful toxin into the blood stream. Death was due to acute paralysis of the heart, and must have been practically instantaneous.'

'Can you tell us what that toxin was?'

'It was a toxin I had never come across before.'

The reporters, listening attentively, wrote down 'Unknown poison'.

'Thank you . . . Mr Henry Winterspoon.'

Mr Winterspoon was a large, dreamy-looking man with a benignant expression. He looked kindly but stupid. It came as something of a shock to learn that he was chief Government analyst and an authority on rare poisons.

The coroner held up the fatal thorn and asked Mr Winterspoon if he recognized it.

'I do. It was sent to me for analysis.'

'Will you tell us the result of that analysis?'

'Certainly. I should say that originally the dart had been dipped in a preparation of native curare – an arrow poison used by certain tribes.'

The reporters wrote with gusto.

'You consider, then, that death may have been due to curare.'

'Oh, no,' said Mr Winterspoon. 'There was only the faintest trace of the original preparation. According to my analysis, the dart had recently been dipped in the venom of *Dispholidus Typus*, better known as the boomslang or tree snake.'

'A boomslang? What is a boomslang?'

'It is a South African snake – one of the most deadly and poisonous in existence. Its effect on a human being is not known, but some idea of the intense virulence of the venom can be realized when I tell you that on injecting the venom into a hyena, the hyena died before the needle could be withdrawn. A jackal died as though shot by a gun. The

45

poison causes acute haemorrhage under the skin and also acts on the heart, paralysing its action.'

The reporters wrote: '*Extraordinary Story. Snake Poison in Air Drama. Deadlier than the Cobra.*'

'Have you ever known the venom to be used in a case of deliberate poisoning?'

'Never. It is most interesting.'

Thank you, Mr Winterspoon.'

Detective-Sergeant Wilson deposed to the finding of the blowpipe behind the cushion of one of the seats. There were no fingerprints on it. Experiments had been made with the dart and the blowpipe. What you might call the range of it was fairly accurate up to about ten yards.

'M. Hercule Poirot.'

There was a little stir of interest, but M. Poirot's evidence was very restrained. He had noticed nothing out of the way. Yes, it was he who had found the tiny dart on the floor of the car. It was in such a position as it would naturally have occupied if it had fallen from the neck of the dead woman.

'The Countess of Horbury.'

The reporters wrote: '*Peer's wife gives evidence in Air Death Mystery*.' Some of them put '. . . *in Snake Poison Mystery*.'

Those who wrote for women's papers put, '*Lady Horbury wore one of the new collegian hats and fox furs*,' or '*Lady Horbury, who is one of the smartest women in town, wore black with one of the new collegian hats*,' or '*Lady Horbury, who before her marriage was Miss Cicely Bland, was smartly dressed in black with one of the new hats* . . .'

Everyone enjoyed looking at the smart and lovely young woman, though her evidence was of the briefest. She had noticed nothing; she had never seen the deceased before.

Venetia Kerr succeeded her, but was definitely less of a thrill.

The indefatigable purveyors of news for women wrote, '*Lord Cottesmore's daughter wore a well-cut coat and skirt with one of the new stocks,*' and noted down the phrase, '*Society Women at Inquest.*'

'James Ryder.'

'You are James Bell Ryder, and your address is 17 Blainberry Avenue, NW?'

'Yes.'

'What is your business or profession?'

'I am managing director of the Ellis Vale Cement Co.'

'Will you kindly examine this blowpipe.' (A pause.) 'Have you ever seen this before?'

'No.'

'You did not see any such thing in anybody's hand on board the *Prometheus*?'

'No.'

'You were sitting in seat No. 4, immediately in front of the deceased?'

'What if I was?'

'Please do not take that tone with me. You were sitting in seat No. 4. From that seat you had a view of practically everyone in the compartment.'

'No, I hadn't. I couldn't see any of the people on my side of the thing. The seats have got high backs.'

'But if one of those people had stepped out into the gangway – into such a position as to be able to aim the blowpipe at the deceased – you would have seen them then?'

'Certainly.'

'And you saw no such thing?'

'No.'

'Did any of the people in front of you move from their seats?'

'Well, the man two seats ahead of me got up and went to the toilet compartment.'

'That was in a direction away from you and from the deceased?'

'Yes.'

'Did he come down the car towards you at all?'

47

'No, he went straight back to his seat.'

'Was he carrying anything in his hand?'

'Nothing at all.'

'You're sure of that?'

'Quite.'

'Did anyone else move from his seat?'

'The chap in front of me. He came the other way, past me to the back of the car.'

'I protest,' squeaked Mr Clancy, springing up from his seat in court. 'That was earlier – much earlier – about one o'clock.'

'Kindly sit down,' said the coroner. 'You will be heard presently. Proceed, Mr Ryder. Did you notice if this gentleman had anything in his hands?'

'I think he had a fountain-pen. When he came back he had an orange book in his hand.'

'Is he the only person who came down the car in your direction? Did you yourself leave your seat?'

'Yes, I went to the toilet compartment – and I didn't have any blowpipe in my hand either.'

'You are adopting a highly improper tone. Stand down.'

Mr Norman Gale, dentist, gave evidence of a negative character. Then the indignant Mr Clancy took the stand.

Mr Clancy was news of a minor kind, several degrees inferior to a Peeress.

'*Mystery Story Writer gives Evidence. Well-known author admits purchase of deadly weapon. Sensation in court.*'

But the sensation was perhaps a little premature.

'Yes, sir,' said Mr Clancy shrilly. 'I did purchase a blowpipe, and what is more, I have brought it with me today. I protest strongly against the inference that the blowpipe with which the crime was committed was my blowpipe. Here is my blowpipe.'

And he produced the blowpipe with a triumphant flourish.

The reporters wrote, '*Second blowpipe in court.*'

The coroner dealt severely with Mr Clancy. He was told that he was here to assist justice, not to rebut totally imaginary charges against himself. Then he was questioned about the occurrences on the *Prometheus*, but with very little result. Mr Clancy, as he explained at totally unnecessary length, had been too bemused with the eccentricities of foreign train services and the difficulties of the twenty-four hour times to have noticed anything at all going on round about him. The whole car might have been shooting snake-venomed darts out of blowpipes for all Mr Clancy would have noticed of the matter.

Miss Jane Grey, hairdresser's assistant, created no flutter among journalistic pens.

The two Frenchmen followed.

M. Armand Dupont deposed that he was on his way to London, where he was to deliver a lecture before the Royal Asiatic Society. He and his son had been very interested in a technical discussion and had noticed very little of what went on round them. He had not noticed the deceased until his attention was attracted by the stir of excitement caused by the discovery of her death.

'Did you know this Madame Morisot or Madame Giselle by sight?'

'No, Monsieur, I had never seen her before.'

'But she is a well-known figure in Paris, is she not?'

Old M. Dupont shrugged his shoulders.

'Not to me. In any case, I am not very much in Paris these days.'

'You have lately returned from the East, I understand?'

'That is so, Monsieur – from Persia.'

'You and your son have travelled a good deal in out-of-the-way parts of the world?'

'Pardon?'

'You have journeyed in wild places?'

'That, yes.'

'Have you ever come across a race of people that used snake venom as an arrow poison?'

This had to be translated, and when M. Dupont understood the question he shook his head vigorously.

'Never – never have I come across anything like that.'

His son followed him. His evidence was a repetition of his father's. He had noticed nothing. He had thought it possible that the deceased had been stung by a wasp, because he had himself been annoyed by one and had finally killed it.

The Duponts were the last witnesses.

The coroner cleared his throat and addressed the jury.

This, he said, was without doubt the most astonishing and incredible case with which he had ever dealt in this court. A woman had been murdered – they could rule out any question of suicide or accident – in mid-air, in a small enclosed space. There was no question of any outside person having committed the crime. The murderer or murderers must be of necessity one of the witnesses they had heard this morning. There was no getting away from that fact, and a very terrible and awful one it was. One of the persons present had been lying in a desperate and abandoned manner.

The manner of the crime was one of unparalleled audacity. In the full view of ten – or twelve, counting the stewards – witnesses, the murderer had placed a blowpipe to his lips and sent the fatal dart on its murderous course through the air and no one had observed the act. It seemed frankly incredible, but there was the evidence of the blowpipe, of the dart found on the floor, of the mark on the deceased's neck and of the medical evidence to show that, incredible or not, it had happened.

In the absence of further evidence incriminating some particular person, he could only direct the jury to return a verdict of murder against a person or persons unknown. Everyone present had denied any knowledge of the deceased woman. It would be the work of the police to find out how and where a connexion lay. In the absence of any motive for the crime he could only advise the verdict he had just mentioned. The jury would now consider the verdict.

A square-faced member of the jury with suspicious eyes leaned forward breathing heavily.

'Can I ask a question, sir?'

'Certainly.'

'You say as how the blowpipe was found down a seat? Whose seat was it?'

The coroner consulted his notes. Sergeant Wilson stepped to his side and murmured:

'Ah, yes. The seat in question was No. 9, a seat occupied by M. Hercule Poirot. M. Poirot, I may say, is a very well-known and respected private detective who has – er – collaborated several times with Scotland Yard.'

The square-faced man transferred his gaze to the face of M. Hercule Poirot. It rested with a far from satisfied expression on the little Belgian's long moustaches.

'Foreigners,' said the eyes of the square-faced man, 'you can't trust foreigners, not even if they *are* hand-and-glove with the police.'

Out loud he said:

'It was this Mr Poirot who picked up the dart, wasn't it?'

'Yes.'

The jury retired. They returned after five minutes, and the foreman handed a piece of paper to the coroner.

'What's all this?' The coroner frowned. 'Nonsense, I can't accept this verdict.'

A few minutes later the amended verdict was returned: 'We find that the deceased came to her death by poison, there being insufficient evidence to show by whom the poison was administered.'

CHAPTER 5

After the Inquest

As Jane left the court after the verdict she found Norman Gale beside her.

He said, 'I wonder what was on that paper that the coroner wouldn't have at any price?'

'I can tell you, I think,' said a voice behind him.

The couple turned, to look into the twinkling eyes of M. Hercule Poirot.

'It was a verdict,' said the little man, 'of wilful murder against *me.*'

'Oh, surely –' cried Jane.

Poirot nodded happily.

'*Mais oui.* As I came out I heard one man say to the other, "That little foreigner – mark my words, *he done it!*" The jury thought the same.'

Jane was uncertain whether to condole or to laugh. She decided on the latter. Poirot laughed in sympathy.

'But, see you,' he said, 'definitely I must set to work and clear my character.'

With a smile and a bow he moved away.

Jane and Norman stared after his retreating figure.

'What an extraordinarily rum little beggar,' said Gale. 'Calls himself a detective. I don't see how *he* could do much detecting. Any criminal could spot him a mile off. I don't see how he *could* disguise himself.'

'Haven't you got a very old-fashioned idea of detectives?' asked Jane. 'All the false beard stuff is very out of date. Nowadays detectives just sit and think out a case psychologically.'

'Rather less strenuous.'

'Physically, perhaps; but of course you need a cool, clear brain.'

'I see. A hot muddled one won't do.'

They both laughed.

'Look here,' said Gale. A slight flush rose in his cheeks and he spoke rather fast. 'Would you mind – I mean, it would be frightfully nice of you – it's a bit late – but how about having some tea with me? I feel – comrades in misfortune – and –'

He stopped. To himself he said:

'What is the matter with you, you fool? Can't you ask a girl to have a cup of tea without stammering and blushing and making an utter ass of yourself? What will the girl think of you?'

Gale's confusion served to accentuate Jane's coolness and self-possession.

'Thank you very much,' she said. 'I *would* like some tea.'

They found a tea-shop and a disdainful waitress with a gloomy manner took their order with an air of doubt as of one who might say: 'Don't blame me if you're disappointed. They *say* we serve teas here, but *I* never heard of it.'

The tea-shop was nearly empty. Its emptiness served to emphasize the intimacy of tea drinking together. Jane peeled off her gloves and looked across the table at her companion. He *was* attractive – those blue eyes and that smile. And he was *nice* too.

'It's a queer show, this murder business,' said Gale, plunging hastily into talk. He was still not quite free from an absurd feeling of embarrassment.

'I know,' said Jane. 'I'm rather worried about it – from the point of view of my job, I mean. I don't know how they'll take it.'

'Ye-es. I hadn't thought of that.'

'Antoine's mayn't like to employ a girl who's been mixed up in a murder case and had to give evidence, and all that.'

'People are queer,' said Norman Gale thoughtfully.

'Life's so – so unfair. A thing like this that isn't your fault at all –' He frowned angrily. 'It's damnable!'

'Well, it hasn't happened yet,' Jane reminded him. 'No good getting hot and bothered about something that hasn't happened. After all, I suppose there is some point in it – I might be the person who murdered her! And when you've murdered one person they say you usually murder a lot more; and it wouldn't be very comfortable having your hair done by a person of that kind.'

'Anyone's only got to look at you to know you couldn't murder anybody,' said Norman, gazing at her earnestly.

'I'm not so sure about that,' said Jane. 'I'd like to murder some of my ladies sometimes – if I could be sure I'd get away with it! There's one in particular – she's got a voice like a corncrake and she grumbles at everything. I really think sometimes that murdering her would be a good deed and not a crime at all. So you see I'm quite criminally minded.'

'Well, you didn't do this particular murder, anyway,' said Gale. '*I* can swear to that.'

'And I can swear *you* didn't do it,' said Jane. 'But that won't help you if your patients think you have.'

'My patients, yes –' Gale looked rather thoughtful. 'I suppose you're right – I hadn't really thought of that. A dentist who might be a homicidal maniac – no, it's not a very alluring prospect.'

He added suddenly and impulsively:

'I say, you don't mind my being a dentist, do you?'

Jane raised her eyebrows.

'I? Mind?'

'What I mean is, there's always something rather – well, *comic* about a dentist. Somehow it's not a romantic profession. Now a doctor everyone takes seriously.'

'Cheer up,' said Jane. 'A dentist is decidedly a cut above a hairdresser's assistant.'

They laughed, and Gale said, 'I feel we're going to be friends. Do you?'

'Yes, I think I do.'

'Perhaps you'll dine with me one night and we might do a show?'

'Thank you.'

There was a pause, and then Gale said:

'How did you like Le Pinet?'

'It was great fun.'

'Had you ever been there before?'

'No, you see –'

Jane, suddenly confidential, came out with the story of the winning Sweep ticket. They agreed together on the general romance and desirability of Sweeps and deplored the attitude of an unsympathetic English Government.

Their conversation was interrupted by a young man in a brown suit who had been hovering uncertainly nearby for some minutes before they noticed him.

Now, however, he lifted his hat and addressed Jane with a certain glib assurance.

'Miss Jane Grey?' he said.

'Yes.'

'I represent the *Weekly Howl*, Miss Grey. I wondered if you would care to do us a short article on this Air Death Murder? Point of view of one of the passengers.'

'I think I'd rather not, thanks.'

'Oh, come now, Miss Grey. We'd pay well for it.'

'How much?' asked Jane.

'Fifty pounds – or, well – perhaps we'd make it a bit more. Say sixty.'

'No,' said Jane. 'I don't think I could. I shouldn't know what to say.'

'That's all right,' said the young man easily. 'You needn't actually *write* the article, you know. One of our fellows will just ask you for a few suggestions and work the whole thing up for you. It won't be the least trouble to you.'

'All the same,' said Jane, 'I'd rather not.'

55

'What about a hundred quid? Look here, I really will make it a hundred; and give us a photograph.'

'No,' said Jane. 'I don't like the idea.'

'So you may as well clear out,' said Norman Gale. 'Miss Grey doesn't want to be worried.'

The young man turned to him hopefully.

'Mr Gale, isn't it?' he said. 'Now look here, Mr Gale, if Miss Grey feels a bit squeamish about it, what about your having a shot? Five hundred words. And we'll pay you the same as I offered Miss Grey – and that's a good bargain, because a woman's account of another woman's murder is better news value. I'm offering you a good chance.'

'I don't want it. I shan't write a word for you.'

'It'll be good publicity apart from the pay. Rising professional man – brilliant career ahead of you – all your patients will read it.'

'That,' said Norman Gale, 'is mostly what I'm afraid of.'

'Well, you can't get anywhere without publicity in these days.'

'Possibly, but it depends on the kind of publicity. I'm hoping that just one or two of my patients may not read the papers and may continue in ignorance of the fact that I've been mixed up in a murder case. Now you've had your answer from both of us. Are you going quietly, or have I got to kick you out of here?'

'Nothing to get annoyed about,' said the young man, quite undisturbed by this threat of violence. 'Good evening, and ring me up at the office if you change your mind. Here's my card.'

He made his way cheerfully out of the tea-shop, thinking to himself as he did so: 'Not too bad. Made quite a decent interview.'

And in truth the next issue of the *Weekly Howl* had an important column on the views of two of the witnesses in the Air Murder Mystery. Miss Jane Grey had declared herself too distressed to talk about the matter. It had been a terrible shock to her and she hated to think about it. Mr Norman Gale had expressed himself at great length on the effect upon a professional man's career of being mixed up in a criminal case, however innocently. Mr Gale had humorously expressed the hope that some of his patients only read the fashion columns and so might not suspect the worst when they came for the ordeal of 'the chair'.

When the young man had departed Jane said:

'I wonder why he didn't go for the more important people?'

'Leaves that to his betters, probably,' said Gale grimly. 'He's probably tried there and failed.'

He sat frowning for a minute or two, then he said:

'Jane (I'm going to call you Jane. You don't mind, do you?) Jane – who do you think really murdered this Giselle woman?'

'I haven't the faintest idea.'

'Have you thought about it? *Really* thought about it?'

'Well, no, I don't suppose I have. I've been thinking about my own part in it, and worrying a little. I haven't really wondered seriously which – which of the others did it. I don't think I'd realized until today that one of them *must* have done it.'

'Yes, the coroner put it very plainly. I know *I* didn't do it, and I know *you* didn't do it, because – well, because I was watching you most of the time.'

'Yes,' said Jane. 'I know *you* didn't do it – for the same reason. And of course I know I didn't do it myself! So it *must* have been one of the others; but I don't know which. I haven't the slightest idea. Have you?'

'No.'

Norman Gale looked very thoughtful. He seemed to be puzzling out some train of thought. Jane went on:

'I don't see how we can have the least idea, either. I mean we didn't *see* anything – at least I didn't. Did you?'

Gale shook his head.

'Not a thing.'

'That's what seems so frightfully odd. I dare say *you* wouldn't have seen anything. You weren't facing that way. But I was. I was looking right along the middle. I mean – I could have been –'

Jane stopped and flushed. She was remembering that her eyes had been mostly fixed on a periwinkle blue pullover, and that her mind, far from being receptive to what was going on around her, had been mainly concerned with the personality of the human being inside the periwinkle blue pullover.

Norman Gale thought:

'I wonder what makes her blush like that . . . She's wonderful . . . I'm going to marry her . . . Yes, I am . . . But it's no good looking too far ahead. I've got to have some good excuse for seeing her often. This murder business will do as well as anything else . . . Besides, I really think it would be as well to do something – that whipper-snapper of a reporter and his publicity . . .'

Aloud he said:

'Let's think about it now. Who killed her? Let's go over all the people. The stewards?'

'No,' said Jane.

'I agree. The women opposite us?'

'I don't suppose anyone like Lady Horbury would go killing people. And the other one, Miss Kerr, well, she's far too county. She wouldn't kill an old Frenchwoman, I'm sure.'

'Only an unpopular MFH? I expect you're not far wrong, Jane. Then there's moustachios, but he seems, according to the coroner's jury, to be the most likely person, so that washes him out. The doctor? That doesn't seem very likely, either.'

'If he'd wanted to kill her he could have used something quite untraceable and nobody would ever have known.'

'Ye-es,' said Norman doubtfully. 'These untraceable, tasteless, odourless poisons are very convenient, but I'm a bit doubtful if they really exist. What about the little man who owned up to having a blowpipe?'

'That's rather suspicious. But he seemed a very nice little man, and he needn't have said he had a blowpipe, so that looks as though he were all right.'

'Then there's Jameson – no – what's his name – Ryder?'

'Yes, it might be him.'

'And the two Frenchmen?'

'That's the most likely of all. They've been to queer places. And of course they may have had some reason we know nothing about. I thought the younger one looked very unhappy and worried.'

'You probably would be worried if you'd committed a murder,' said Norman Gale grimly.

'He looked nice, though,' said Jane; 'and the old father was rather a dear. I hope it isn't them.'

'We don't seem to be getting on very fast,' said Norman Gale.

'I don't see how we can get on without knowing a lot of things about the old woman who was murdered. Enemies, and who inherits her money, and all that.'

Norman Gale said thoughtfully:

'You think this is mere idle speculation?'

Jane said coolly, 'Isn't it?'

'Not quite.' Gale hesitated, then went on slowly, 'I have a feeling it may be useful –'

Jane looked at him inquiringly.

'Murder,' said Norman Gale, 'doesn't concern the victim and the guilty only. It affects the innocent too. You and I are innocent, but the shadow of murder has touched us. We don't know how that shadow is going to affect our lives.'

Jane was a person of cool common sense, but she shivered suddenly.

'Don't,' she said. 'You make me feel afraid.'

'I'm a little afraid myself,' said Gale.

CHAPTER 6

Consultation

Hercule Poirot rejoined his friend Inspector Japp. The latter had a grin on his face.

'Hullo, old boy,' he said. 'You've had a pretty near squeak of being locked up in a police cell.'

'I fear,' said Poirot gravely, 'that such an occurrence might have damaged me professionally.'

'Well,' said Japp with a grin, 'detectives do turn out to be criminals sometimes – in story books.'

A tall thin man with an intelligent, melancholy face joined them, and Japp introduced him.

'This is Monsieur Fournier of the Sûreté. He has come over to collaborate with us about this business.'

'I think I have had the pleasure of meeting you once some years ago, M. Poirot,' said Fournier, bowing and shaking hands. 'I have also heard of you from M. Giraud.'

A very faint smile seemed to hover on his lips. And Poirot, who could well imagine the terms in which Giraud (whom he himself had been in the habit of referring to disparagingly as the 'human fox-hound') had spoken of him, permitted himself a small discreet smile in reply.

'I suggest,' said Poirot, 'that both you gentlemen should dine with me at my rooms. I have already invited Maître Thibault. That is, if you and my friend Japp do not object to my collaboration.'

'That's all right, old cock,' said Japp, slapping him heartily on the back. 'You're in on this on the ground floor.'

'We shall be indeed honoured,' murmured the Frenchman ceremoniously.

'You see,' said Poirot, 'as I said to a very charming young lady just now, I am anxious to clear my character.'

'That jury certainly didn't like the look of you,' agreed Japp with a renewal of his grin. 'Best joke I've heard for a long time.'

By common consent no mention of the case was made during the very excellent meal which the little Belgian provided for his friends.

'After all, it *is* possible to eat well in England,' murmured Fournier appreciatively as he made delicate use of a thoughtfully provided toothpick.

'A delicious meal, M. Poirot,' said Thibault.

'Bit Frenchified, but damn good,' pronounced Japp.

'A meal should always lie lightly on the *estomac*,' said Poirot. 'It should not be so heavy as to paralyse thought.'

'I can't say my stomach ever gives me much trouble,' said Japp. 'But I won't argue the point. Well, we'd better get down to business. I know that M. Thibault has got an appointment this evening, so I suggest that we should start by consulting him on any point that seems likely to be useful.'

'I am at your service, gentlemen. Naturally I can speak more freely here than in a coroner's court. I had a hurried conversation with Inspector Japp before the inquest, and he indicated a policy of reticence – the bare necessary facts.'

'Quite right,' said Japp. 'Don't ever spill the beans too soon. But now let's hear all you can tell us of this Giselle woman.'

'To speak the truth, I know very little. I know her as the world knew her – as a public character. Of her private life as an individual I know very little. Probably M. Fournier here can tell you more than I can. But I will say to you this: Madame Giselle was what you call in this country "a character". She was unique. Of her antecedents nothing is known. I have an idea that as a young woman she was good-looking. I believe that as a result of smallpox she lost her looks. She was – I am giving you my impressions – a woman who enjoyed power; she had power. She was a keen woman of

61

business. She was the type of hard-headed Frenchwoman who would never allow sentiment to affect her business interests; but she had the reputation of carrying on her profession with scrupulous honesty.'

He looked for assent to Fournier. That gentleman nodded his dark melancholic head.

'Yes,' he said. 'She was honest – according to her lights. Yet the law could have called her to account if only evidence had been forthcoming; but that –' He shrugged his shoulders despondently. 'It is too much to ask, with human nature what it is.'

'You mean?'

'*Chantage.*'

'Blackmail?' echoed Japp.

'Yes, blackmail of a peculiar and specialized kind. It was Madame Giselle's custom to lend money on what I think you call in this country "note of hand alone". She used her discretion as to the sums she lent and the methods of repayment; but I may tell you that she had her own methods of getting paid.'

Poirot leaned forward interestedly.

'As Maître Thibault said today, Madame Giselle's clientèle lay amongst the upper and professional classes. Those classes are particularly vulnerable to the force of public opinion. Madame Giselle had her own intelligence service . . . It was her custom before lending money (that is, in the case of a large sum) to collect as many facts as possible about the client in question; and her intelligence system, I may say, was an extraordinarily good one. I will echo what our friend has said: according to her lights Madame Giselle was scrupulously honest. She kept faith with those who kept faith with her. I honestly believe that she has never made use of her secret knowledge to obtain money from anyone unless that money was already owed to her.'

'You mean,' said Poirot, 'that this secret knowledge was her form of security?'

'Exactly; and in using it she was perfectly ruthless and deaf to any finer shades of feeling; and I will tell you this, gentlemen: *her system paid!* Very, very rarely did she have to write off a bad debt. A man or woman in a prominent position would go to desperate lengths to obtain the money which would obviate a public scandal. As I say, we knew of her activities; but as for prosecution –' He shrugged his shoulders. 'That is a more difficult matter. Human nature is human nature.'

'And supposing,' said Poirot, 'that she did, as you say happened occasionally, have to write off a bad debt – what then?'

'In that case,' said Fournier slowly, 'the information she held was published, or was given to the person concerned in the matter.'

There was a moment's silence. Then Poirot said:

'Financially, that did not benefit her?'

'No,' said Fournier – 'not directly, that is.'

'But indirectly?'

'Indirectly,' said Japp, 'it made the others pay up, eh?'

'Exactly,' said Fournier. 'It was valuable for what you call the moral effect.'

'Immoral effect, I should call it,' said Japp. 'Well' – he rubbed his nose thoughtfully – 'it opens up a very pretty line in motives for murder – a very pretty line. Then there's the question of who is going to come into her money.' He appealed to Thibault. 'Can you help us there at all?'

'There was a daughter,' said the lawyer. 'She did not live with her mother – indeed I fancy that her mother has never seen her since she was a tiny child; but she made a will many years ago now leaving everything, with the exception of a small legacy to her maid, to her daughter Anne Morisot. As far as I know she has never made another.'

'And her fortune is large?' asked Poirot.

The lawyer shrugged his shoulders.

'At a guess eight or nine million francs.'

Poirot pursed his lips to a whistle. Japp said, 'Lord, she didn't look it. Let me see, what's the exchange – that's – why, that must be well over a hundred thousand pounds. Whew!'

'Mademoiselle Anne Morisot will be a very wealthy young woman,' said Poirot.

'Just as well she wasn't on that plane,' said Japp drily. 'She might have been suspected of bumping off her mother to get the dibs. How old would she be?'

'I really cannot say. I should imagine about twenty-four or five.'

'Well, there doesn't seem anything to connect her with the crime. We'll have to get down to this blackmailing business. Everyone on that plane denies knowing Madame Giselle. One of them is lying. We've got to find out which. An examination of her private papers might help, eh, Fournier?'

'My friend,' said the Frenchman, 'immediately the news came through, after I had conversed with Scotland Yard on the telephone, I went straight to her house. There was a safe there containing papers. All those papers had been burnt.'

'Burnt? Who by? Why?'

'Madame Giselle had a confidential maid, Elise. Elise had instructions in the event of anything happening to her mistress to open the safe (the combination of which she knew) and burn the contents.'

'What? But that's amazing!' Japp stared.

'You see,' said Fournier, 'Madame Giselle had her own code. She kept faith with those who kept faith with her. She gave her promise to her clients that she would deal honestly with them. She was ruthless, but she was also a woman of her word.'

Japp shook his head dumbly. The four men were silent, ruminating on the strange character of the dead woman . . .

Maître Thibault rose.

'I must leave you, Messieurs. I have to keep an appointment. If there is any further information I can give you at any time, you know my address.'

He shook hands with them ceremoniously and left the apartment.

CHAPTER 7

Probabilities

With the departure of Maître Thibault, the three men drew their chairs a little closer to the table.

'Now, then,' said Japp, 'let's get down to it.' He unscrewed the cap of his fountain-pen. 'There were eleven passengers in that plane – in the rear car, I mean; the other doesn't come into it – eleven passengers and two stewards – that's thirteen people we've got. *One of the remaining twelve did the old woman in.* Some of the passengers were English, some were French. The latter I shall hand over to M. Fournier. The English ones I'll take on. Then there are inquiries to be made in Paris – that's your job too, Fournier.'

'And not only in Paris,' said Fournier. 'In the summer Giselle did a lot of business at the French watering-places – Deauville, Le Pinet, Wimereux. She went down south too, to Antibes and Nice, and all those places.'

'A good point; one or two of the people in the *Prometheus* mentioned Le Pinet, I remember. Well, that's one line. Then we've got to get down to the actual murder itself – prove who could possibly be in a position to use that blowpipe.' He unrolled a large sketch plan of the car of the aeroplane and placed it in the centre of the table. 'Now, then, we're ready for the preliminary work. And, to begin with, let's go through the people one by one, and decide on the probabilities and – even more important – the possibilities.

'To begin with, we can eliminate M. Poirot here. That brings the number down to eleven.'

Poirot shook his head sadly.

'You are of too trustful a nature, my friend. You should trust nobody – nobody at all.'

'Well, we'll leave you in if you like,' said Japp good-temperedly. 'Then there are the stewards. Seems to me very unlikely it should be either of them from the probability point of view. They're not likely to have borrowed money on a grand scale and they've both got a good record – decent, sober men, both of them. It would surprise me very much if either of them had anything to do with this. On the other hand, from the possibility point of view we've got to include them. They were up and down the car. They could actually have taken up a position from which they could have used that blowpipe – from the right angle, I mean – though I don't believe that a steward could shoot a poisoned dart out of a blowpipe in a car full of people without someone noticing him do it. I know by experience that most people are blind as bats; but there are limits. Of course, in a way, the same thing applies to every blessed person. It was madness, absolute madness, to commit a crime that way. Only about a chance in a hundred that it would come off without being spotted. The fellow that did it must have had the luck of the devil. Of all the damn fool ways to commit a murder –'

Poirot, who had been sitting with his eyes down, smoking quietly, interposed a question.

'You think it was a foolish way of committing a murder, yes?'

'Of course it was. It was absolute madness.'

'And yet – it *succeeded*. We sit here, we three, we talk about it, but we have no knowledge of *who committed the crime*! That is success!'

'That's pure luck,' argued Japp. 'The murderer ought to have been spotted five or six times over.'

Poirot shook his head in a dissatisfied manner.

Fournier looked at him curiously.

'What is it that is in your mind, M. Poirot?'

'*Mon ami*,' said Poirot, 'my point is this: an affair must be judged by its results. This affair has succeeded. That is my point.'

'And yet,' said the Frenchman thoughtfully, 'it seems almost a miracle.'

'Miracle or no miracle, there it is,' said Japp. 'We've got the medical evidence, we've got the weapon; and if anyone had told me a week ago that I should be investigating a crime where a woman was killed with a poisoned dart with snake venom on it – well, I'd have laughed in his face! It's an insult – that's what this murder is – an insult.'

He breathed deeply. Poirot smiled.

'It is, perhaps, a murder committed by a person with a perverted sense of humour,' said Fournier thoughtfully. 'It is most important in a crime to get an idea of the psychology of the murderer.'

Japp snorted slightly at the word psychology, which he disliked and mistrusted.

'That's the sort of stuff M. Poirot likes to hear,' he said.

'I am very interested, yes, in what you both say.'

'You don't doubt that she was killed that way, I suppose?' Japp asked him suspiciously. 'I know your tortuous mind.'

'No, no, my friend. My mind is quite at ease on that point. The poisoned thorn that I picked up was the cause of death – that is quite certain. But nevertheless there are points about this case –'

He paused, shaking his head perplexedly.

Japp went on:

'Well, to get back to our Irish stew, we can't wash out the stewards absolutely, but I think myself it's very unlikely that either of them had anything to do with it. Do you agree, M. Poirot?'

'Oh, you remember what I said. Me – I would not wash out – what a term, *mon Dieu*! – anybody at this stage.'

'Have it your own way. Now, the passengers. Let's start up the end by the stewards' pantry and the toilets. Seat No. 16.' He jabbed a pencil on the plan. 'That's the hairdressing girl, Jane Grey. Got a ticket in the Irish Sweep – blued it at Le Pinet. That means the girl's a gambler. She *might* have been hard-up and borrowed from the old dame – doesn't seem likely, either, that she borrowed a large sum, or that Giselle could have a "hold" over her. Seems rather too small a fish for what we're looking for. And I don't think a hairdresser's assistant had the remotest chance of laying her hands on snake venom. They don't use it as a hair dye or for face massage.

'In a way it was rather a mistake to use snake venom; it narrows things down a lot. Only about two people in a hundred would be likely to have any knowledge of it and be able to lay hands on the stuff.'

'Which makes one thing, at least, perfectly clear,' said Poirot.

It was Fournier who shot a quick glance of inquiry at him.

Japp was busy with his own ideas.

'I look at it like this,' he said: 'The murderer has got to fall into one of two categories: either he's a man who's knocked about the world in queer places – a man who knows something of snakes and of the more deadly varieties and of the habits of the native tribes who use the venom to dispose of their enemies – that's category No. 1.'

'And the other?'

'The scientific line. Research. This boomslang stuff is the kind of thing they experiment with in high-class laboratories. I had a talk with Winterspoon. Apparently snake venom – cobra venom, to be exact – is sometimes used in medicine. It's used in the treatment of epilepsy with a fair amount of success. There's a lot being done in the way of scientific investigation into snake bite.'

'Interesting and suggestive,' said Fournier.

'Yes, but let's go on. Neither of those categories fit the Grey girl. As far as she's concerned, motive seems unlikely, chances of getting the poison – poor. Actual possibility of doing the blowpipe act very doubtful indeed – almost impossible. See here.'

69

The three men bent over the plan.

'Here's 16,' said Japp. 'And here's 2, where Giselle was sitting with a lot of people and seats intervening. If the girl didn't move from her seat – and everybody says she didn't – she couldn't possibly have aimed the thorn to catch Giselle on the side of the neck. I think we can take it she's pretty well out of it.

'Now then, 12, opposite. That's the dentist, Norman Gale. Very much the same applies to him. Small fry. I suppose he'd have a slightly better chance of getting hold of snake venom.'

'It is not an injection usually favoured by dentists,' murmured Poirot gently. 'It would be a case of kill rather than cure.'

'A dentist has enough fun with his patients as it is,' said Japp, grinning. 'Still, I suppose he might move in circles where you could get access to some funny business in drugs. He might have a scientific friend. But as regards *possibility* he's pretty well out of it. He *did* leave his seat, but only to go to the toilet – that's in the opposite direction. On his way back to his seat he couldn't be farther than the gangway here, and to shoot off a thorn from a blowpipe so as to catch the old lady in the neck he'd have to have a kind of pet thorn that would do tricks and make a right-angle turn. So *he's* pretty well out of it.'

'I agree,' said Fournier. 'Let us proceed.'

'We'll cross the gangway now. 17.'

'That was my seat originally,' said Poirot. 'I yielded it to one of the ladies since she desired to be near her friend.'

'That's the Honourable Venetia. Well, what about her? She's a big bug. She might have borrowed from Giselle. Doesn't look as though she had any guilty secrets in her life – but perhaps she pulled a horse in a point-to-point, or whatever they call it. We'll have to pay a little attention to her. The *position's* possible. If Giselle had got her head turned a little looking out of the window the Hon. Venetia

70

could take a sporting shot (or do you call it a sporting puff?) diagonally across down the car. It would be a bit of a fluke, though. I rather think she'd have to stand up to do it. She's the sort of woman who goes out with the guns in the autumn. I don't know whether shooting with a gun is any help to you with a native blowpipe? I suppose it's a question of eye just the same – eye and practice; and she's probably got friends – men – who've been big-game hunting in odd parts of the globe. She might have got hold of some queer native stuff that way. What balderdash it all sounds, though! It doesn't make *sense*.'

'It does indeed seem unlikely,' said Fournier. 'Mademoiselle Kerr – I saw her at the inquest today –' He shook his head. 'One does not readily connect her with murder.'

'Seat 13,' said Japp. 'Lady Horbury. *She's* a bit of a dark horse. I know something about her I'll tell you presently. I shouldn't be surprised if she had a guilty secret or two.'

'I happen to know,' said Fournier, 'that the lady in question has been losing very heavily at the baccarat table at Le Pinet.'

'That's smart of you. Yes, she's the type of pigeon to be mixed up with Giselle.'

'I agree absolutely.'

'Very well, then – so far, so good. *But how did she do it?* She didn't leave her seat either, you remember. She'd have had to have knelt up in her seat and leaned over the top – with ten people looking at her. Oh, hell, let's get on.'

'9 and 10,' said Fournier, moving his finger on the plan.

'M. Hercule Poirot and Dr Bryant,' said Japp. 'What has M. Poirot to say for himself?'

Poirot shook his head sadly.

'*Mon estomac*,' he said pathetically. 'Alas, that the brain should be the servant of the stomach.'

'I, too,' said Fournier with sympathy. 'In the air I do not feel well.'

He closed his eyes and shook his head expressively.

'Now then, Dr Bryant. What about Dr Bryant? Big bug in Harley Street. Not very likely to go to a French woman moneylender; but you never know. And if any funny business crops up with a doctor he's done for life! Here's where my scientific theory comes in. A man like Bryant, at the top of the tree, is in with all the medical research people. He could pinch a test-tube of snake venom as easy as winking when he happens to be in some swell laboratory.'

'They check these things, my friend,' objected Poirot. 'It would not be just like plucking a buttercup in a meadow.'

'Even if they do check 'em, a clever man could substitute something harmless. It could be done, simply because a man like Bryant would be above suspicion.'

'There is much in what you say,' agreed Fournier.

'The only thing is, why did he draw attention to the thing? Why not say the woman died from heart failure – natural death?'

Poirot coughed. The other two looked at him inquiringly.

'I fancy,' he said, 'that that was the doctor's first – well, shall we say impression? After all, it looked very like natural death, possibly as the result of a wasp sting; there was a wasp, remember –'

'Not likely to forget that wasp,' put in Japp. 'You're always harping on it.'

'However,' continued Poirot, '*I* happened to notice the fatal thorn on the ground and picked it up. Once we had found that, everything pointed to murder.'

'The thorn would be bound to be found anyway.'

Poirot shook his head.

'There is just a chance that the murderer might have been able to pick it up unobserved.'

'Bryant?'

'Bryant or another.'

'H'm – rather risky.'

Fournier disagreed.

72

'You think so now,' he said, 'because you know that it is murder. But when a lady dies suddenly of heart failure, if a man is to drop his handkerchief and stoop to pick it up, who will notice the action or think twice about it?'

'That's true,' agreed Japp. 'Well, I fancy Bryant is definitely on the list of suspects. He could lean his head round the corner of his seat and do the blowpipe act – again diagonally across the car. But why nobody saw him –! However, I won't go into that again. Whoever did it *wasn't* seen!'

'And for that, I fancy, there must be a reason,' said Fournier. 'A reason that, by all I have heard,' he smiled, 'will appeal to M. Poirot. I mean a psychological reason.'

'Continue, my friend,' said Poirot. 'It is interesting what you say there.'

'Supposing,' said Fournier, 'that when travelling in a train you were to pass a house in flames. Everyone's eyes would at once be drawn to the window. Everyone would have their attention fixed on a certain point. A man in such a moment might whip out a dagger and stab a man, and nobody would see him do it.'

'That is true,' said Poirot. 'I remember a case in which I was concerned – a case of poison, where that very point arose. There was, as you call it, a psychological moment. If we discover that there was such a moment during the journey of the *Prometheus* –'

'We ought to find that out by questioning the stewards and the passengers,' said Japp.

'True. But if there *was* such a psychological moment, it must follow logically that the *cause* of that moment must have originated with the murderer. He must have been able to produce the particular effect that caused that moment.'

'Perfectly, perfectly,' said the Frenchman.

'Well, we'll note down that as a point for questions,' said Japp. 'I'm coming now to seat No. 8 – Daniel Michael Clancy.'

Japp spoke the name with a certain amount of relish.

'In my opinion he's the most likely suspect we've got. What's easier than for a mystery author to fake up an interest in snake venom and get some unsuspecting scientific chemist to let him handle the stuff? Don't forget he went down past Giselle's seat – the only one of the passengers who did.'

'I assure you, my friend,' said Poirot, 'that I have not forgotten that point.'

He spoke with emphasis.

Japp went on:

'He could have used that blowpipe from fairly close quarters without any need of a "psychological moment", as you call it. And he stood quite a respectable chance of getting away with it. Remember, he knows all about blowpipes – he said so.'

'Which makes one pause, perhaps.'

'Sheer artfulness,' said Japp. 'And as to this blowpipe he produced today, who is to say that it's the one he bought two years ago? The whole thing looks very fishy to me. I don't think it's healthy for a man to be always brooding over crime and detective stories, reading up all sorts of cases. It puts ideas into his head.'

'It is certainly necessary for a writer to have ideas in his head,' agreed Poirot.

Japp returned to his plan of the plane.

'No. 4 was Ryder – the seat slap in front of the dead woman. Don't think he did it. But we can't leave him out. He went to the toilet. He could have taken a pot shot on the way back from fairly close quarters; the only thing is he'd be right up against the archaeologist fellows when he did so. They'd notice it – couldn't help it.'

Poirot shook his head thoughtfully.

'You are not, perhaps, acquainted with many archaeologists? If these two were having a really absorbing discussion on some point at issue – *eh bien*, my friend, their concentration would be such that they would be quite blind and deaf to the outside world. They would be existing, you see, in five thousand or so BC. Nineteen hundred and thirty-five AD would have been non-existent for them.'

Japp looked a little sceptical.

'Well, we'll pass on to them. What can you tell us about the Duponts, Fournier?'

'M. Armand Dupont is one of the most distinguished archaeologists in France.'

'Then that doesn't get us anywhere much. Their position in the car is pretty good from my point of view – across the gangway but slightly farther forward than Giselle. And I suppose that they've knocked about the world and dug things up in a lot of queer places; they might easily have got hold of some native snake poison.'

'It is possible, yes,' said Fournier.

'But you don't believe it's likely?'

Fournier shook his head doubtfully.

'M. Dupont lives for his profession. He is an enthusiast. He was formerly an antique dealer. He gave up a flourishing business to devote himself to excavation. Both he and his son are devoted heart and soul to their profession. It seems to me unlikely – I will not say impossible, since the ramifications of the Stavisky business I will believe anything – *unlikely* that they are mixed up in this business.'

'All right,' said Japp.

He picked up the sheet of paper on which he had been making notes and cleared his throat.

'This is where we stand. *Jane Grey*. Probability – poor. Possibility – practically nil. *Gale*. Probability – poor. Possibility – again practically nil. *Miss Kerr*. Very improbable. Possibility – doubtful. *Lady Horbury*. Probability – good. Possibility – practically nil. *M. Poirot* – almost certainly the criminal; the only man on board who could create a psychological moment.'

Japp enjoyed a good laugh over his little joke, and Poirot smiled indulgently and Fournier a trifle diffidently. Then the detective resumed:

75

'*Bryant*. Probability and possibility – both good. *Clancy*. Motive doubtful – probability and possibility very good indeed. *Ryder*. Probability uncertain – possibility quite fair. *The two Duponts*. Probability poor as regards motive – good as to means of obtaining poison. Possibility – good.

'That's a pretty fair summary, I think, as far as we can go. We'll have to do a lot of routine inquiry. I shall take on Clancy and Bryant first – find out what they've been up to – if they've been hard up at any time in the past – if they've seemed worried or upset lately – their movements in the last year – all that sort of stuff. I'll do the same for Ryder. Then it won't do to neglect the others entirely. I'll get Wilson to nose round there. M. Fournier here will undertake the Duponts.'

The man from the Sûreté nodded.

'Be well assured – that will be attended to. I shall return to Paris tonight. There may be something to be got out of Elise, Giselle's maid, now that we know a little more about the case. Also, I will check up Giselle's movements very carefully. It will be well to know where she has been during the summer. She was, I know, at Le Pinet once or twice. We may get information as to her contacts with some of the English people involved. Ah, yes, there is much to do.'

They both looked at Poirot, who was absorbed in thought.

'You going to take a hand at all, M. Poirot?' asked Japp.

Poirot roused himself.

'Yes, I think I should like to accompany M. Fournier to Paris.'

'*Enchanté*,' said the Frenchman.

'What are you up to, I wonder?' said Japp. He looked at Poirot curiously. 'You've been very quiet over all this. Got some of your little ideas, eh?'

'One or two, one or two; but it is very difficult.'

'Let's hear about it.'

'One thing that worries me,' said Poirot slowly, 'is the place where the blowpipe was found.'

76

'Naturally! It nearly got you locked up.'

Poirot shook his head.

'I do not mean that. It is not because it was found pushed down beside my seat that it worries me – it was its being pushed down behind any seat.'

'I don't see anything in that,' said Japp. 'Whoever did it had got to hide the thing somewhere. He couldn't risk its being found on him.'

'*Evidemment*. But you may have noticed, my friend, when you examined the plane, that although the windows cannot be opened, there is in each of them a ventilator – a circle of small round holes in the glass which can be opened or closed by turning a fan of glass. Those holes are of a sufficient circumference to admit of the passage of our blowpipe. What could be simpler than to get rid of the blowpipe that way? It falls to the earth beneath, and it is extremely unlikely that it will ever be found.'

'I can think of an objection to that – the murderer was afraid of being seen. If he pushed the blowpipe through the ventilator someone might have noticed.'

'I see,' said Poirot. 'He was not afraid of being seen placing the blowpipe to his lips and dispatching the fatal dart, but he *was* afraid of being seen trying to push the blowpipe through the window!'

'Sounds absurd, I admit,' said Japp; 'but there it is. He *did* hide the blowpipe behind the cushion of a seat. We can't get away from that.'

Poirot did not answer, and Fournier asked curiously:

'It gives you an idea, that?'

Poirot bowed his head assentingly.

'It gives rise to, say, a speculation in my mind.'

With absent-minded fingers he straightened the unused inkstand that Japp's impatient hand had set a little askew.

Then lifting his head sharply, he asked:

'*A propos*, have you that detailed list of the belongings of the passengers that I asked you to get me?'

CHAPTER 8

The List

'I'm a man of my word, I am,' said Japp.

He grinned and dived his hand into his pocket, bringing out a mass of closely-typewritten paper.

'Here you are. It's all here – down to the minutest detail! And I'll admit that there is one rather curious thing in it. I'll talk to you about it when you've finished reading the stuff.'

Poirot spread out the sheets on the table and began to read. Fournier moved up and read them over his shoulder:

'*James Ryder*.

'*Pockets*. – Linen handkerchief marked J. Pigskin notecase – seven £1 notes, three business cards. Letter from partner George Ebermann hoping "loan has been successfully negotiated . . . otherwise we're in Queer Street". Letter signed Maudie making appointment Trocadero following evening (cheap paper, illiterate handwriting). Silver cigarette-case. Match-folder. Fountain-pen. Bunch of keys. Yale door key. Loose change in French and English money.

'*Attaché Case*. – Mass of papers concerning dealings in cement. Copy of *Bootless Cup* (banned in this country). A box of "Immediate Cold Cures".

'*Dr Bryant*.

'*Pockets*. – Two linen handkerchiefs. Notecase containing £20 and 500 francs. Loose change in French and English money. Engagement book. Cigarette-case. Lighter. Fountain-pen. Yale door key. Bunch of keys.

'Flute in case.

'Carrying *Memoirs of Benvenuto Cellini* and *Les Maux de l'Oreille*.

'*Norman Gale*.

'*Pockets*. – Silk handkerchief. Wallet containing £1 in

English and 600 francs. Loose change. Business cards of two French firms – makers of dental instruments. Bryant & May matchbox – empty. Silver lighter. Briar pipe. Rubber tobacco pouch. Yale door key.

'*Attaché Case*. – White linen coat. Two small dental mirrors. Dental rolls of cottonwool. *La Vie Parisienne*. *The Strand Magazine*. *The Autocar*.

'*Armand Dupont*.

'*Pockets*. – Wallet containing 1000 francs and £10 in English. Spectacles in case. Loose change in French money. Cotton handkerchief. Packet of cigarettes, match-folder. Cards in case. Toothpick.

'*Attaché Case*. – Manuscript of proposed address to Royal Asiatic Society. Two German archaeological publications. Two sheets of rough sketches of pottery. Ornamented hollow tubes (said to be Kurdish pipe stems). Small basketwork tray. Nine unmounted photographs – all of pottery.

'*Jean Dupont*.

'*Pockets*. – Notecase containing £5 in English and 300 francs. Cigarette-case. Cigarette-holder (ivory). Lighter. Fountain-pen. Two pencils. Small notebook full of scribbled notes. Letter in English from L. Marriner giving invitation to lunch at restaurant near Tottenham Court Road. Loose change in French.

'*Daniel Clancy*.

'*Pockets*. – Handkerchief (ink-stained). Fountain-pen (leaking). Notecase containing £4 and 100 francs. Three newspaper cuttings dealing with recent crimes (one poisoning by arsenic and two embezzlement). Two letters from house agents with details of country properties. Engagement book. Four pencils. Pen-knife. Three receipted and four unpaid bills. Letter from "Gordon" headed S.S. *Minotaur*. Half done crossword puzzle cut from *Times*. Notebook containing suggestions for plots. Loose change in Italian, French, Swiss and English money. Receipted hotel bill, Naples. Large bunch of keys.

'*In overcoat pocket.* – Manuscript notes of *Murder on Vesuvius*. Continental Bradshaw. Golf ball. Pair of socks. Toothbrush. Receipted hotel bill, Paris.

'*Miss Kerr.*

'*Vanity bag.* – Lipstick. Two cigarette-holders (one ivory and one jade). Flapjack. Cigarette-case. Match-folder. Handkerchief. £2 English. Loose change. One half letter of credit. Keys.

'*Dressing-case.* – Shagreen fitted. Bottles, brushes, combs, etc. Manicure outfit. Washing bag containing toothbrush, sponge, toothpowder, soap. Two pairs of scissors. Five letters from family and friends in England. Two Tauchnitz novels. Photograph of two spaniels.

'Carried *Vogue* and *Good Housekeeping*.

'*Miss Grey.*

'*Handbag.* – Lipstick, rouge, flapjack. Yale key and one trunk key. Pencil. Cigarette-case. Holder. Match-folder. Two handkerchiefs. Receipted hotel bill, Le Pinet. Small book, *French Phrases*. Notecase, 100 francs and 10s. Loose French and English change. One Casino counter value 5 francs.

'*In pocket of travelling coat.* – Six postcards of Paris, two handkerchiefs and silk scarf. Letter signed "Gladys". Tube of aspirin.

'*Lady Horbury.*

'*Vanity bag.* – Two lipsticks, rouge, flapjack. Handkerchief. Three *mille* notes. £6 English. Loose change (French). A diamond ring. Five French stamps. Two cigarette-holders. Lighter with case.

'*Dressing-case.* – Complete makeup outfit. Elaborate manicure set (gold). Small bottle labelled (in ink) Boracic Powder.'

As Poirot came to the end of the list, Japp laid his finger on the last item.

'Rather smart of our man. He thought that didn't seem quite in keeping with the rest. Boracic powder my eye! The white powder in that bottle was cocaine.'

Poirot's eyes opened a little. He nodded his head slowly.

'Nothing much to do with our case, perhaps,' said Japp. 'But you don't need me to tell you that a woman who's got the cocaine habit hasn't got much moral restraint. I've an idea anyway that her ladyship wouldn't stick at much to get what she wanted, in spite of all that helpless feminine business. All the same, I doubt if she'd have the nerve to carry a thing like this through; and, frankly, I can't see that it was *possible* for her to do it. The whole thing is a bit of a teaser.'

Poirot gathered up the loose typewritten sheets and read them through once again. Then he laid them down with a sigh.

'On the face of it,' he said, 'it seems to point very plainly to one person as having committed the crime. And yet, I cannot see *why*, or even *how*.'

Japp stared at him.

'Are you pretending that by reading all this stuff you've got an idea who did it?'

'I think so.'

Japp seized the papers from him and read them through, handing each sheet over to Fournier as he had finished with it. Then he slapped them down on the table and stared at Poirot.

'Are you pulling my leg, Moosior Poirot?'

'No, no. *Quelle idée!*'

The Frenchman in his turn laid down the sheets.

'What about you, Fournier?'

The Frenchman shook his head. 'I may be stupid,' he said, 'but I cannot see that this list advances us much.'

'Not by itself,' said Poirot. 'But taken in conjunction with certain features of the case, no? Well, it may be that I am wrong – quite wrong.'

'Well, come out with your theory,' said Japp. 'I'll be interested to hear it at all events.'

Poirot shook his head.

'No, as you say it is a theory – a theory only. I hoped to find a certain object on that list. *Eh bien*, I have found it. It is there; but it seems to point in the wrong direction. The right clue on the wrong person. That means there is much work to be done,

81

and truly there is much that is still obscure to me. I cannot see my way; only certain facts seem to stand out, to arrange themselves in a significant pattern. You do not find it so? No, I see you do not. Let us then each work to his own idea. I have no *certainty*, I tell you, only a certain suspicion . . .'

'I believe you're just talking through your hat,' said Japp. He rose. 'Well, let's call it a day. I work the London end, you return to Paris, Fournier – and what about our M. Poirot?'

'I still wish to accompany M. Fournier to Paris – more than ever now.'

'More than ever –? I'd like to know just what kind of maggot you've got in your brain.'

'Maggot? *Ce n'est pas joli, ça!*'

Fournier shook hands ceremoniously.

'I wish you good evening, with many thanks for your delightful hospitality. We will meet then at Croydon tomorrow morning?'

'Exactly. *A demain.*'

'Let us hope,' said Fournier, 'that nobody will murder us *en route*.'

The two detectives departed.

Poirot remained for a time as in a dream. Then he rose, cleared away any traces of disorder, emptied the ashtrays and straightened the chairs.

He went to a side table and picked up a copy of the *Sketch*. He turned the pages until he came to the one he sought.

'Two Sun Worshippers,' it was headed. 'The Countess of Horbury and Mr Raymond Barraclough at Le Pinet.' He looked at the two laughing figures in bathing-dresses, their arms entwined.

'I wonder,' said Hercule Poirot. 'One might do something along those lines . . . Yes, one might.'

CHAPTER 9

Elise Grandier

The weather on the following day was of so perfect a nature that even Hercule Poirot had to admit that his *estomac* was perfectly peaceful.

On this occasion they were travelling by the 8.45 Air Service to Paris.

There were seven or eight travellers beside Poirot and Fournier in the compartment, and the Frenchman utilized the journey to make some experiments. He took from his pocket a small piece of bamboo and three times during the journey he raised this to his lips, pointing it in a certain direction. Once he did it bending himself round the corner of his seat, once with his head slightly turned sideways, once when he was returning from the toilet compartment; and on each occasion he caught the eye of some passenger or other eyeing him with mild astonishment. On the last occasion, indeed, every eye in the car seemed to be fixed upon him.

Fournier sank in his seat discouraged, and was but little cheered by observing Poirot's open amusement.

'You are amused, my friend? But you agree one must try experiments?'

'*Evidemment!* In truth I admire your thoroughness. There is nothing like ocular demonstration. You play the part of the murderer with blowpipe. The result is perfectly clear. Everybody sees you!'

'Not *everybody*.'

'In a sense, no. On each occasion there is *somebody* who does *not* see you; but for a successful murder that is not enough. You must be reasonably sure that *nobody* will see you.'

'And that is impossible given ordinary conditions,' said Fournier. 'I hold then to my theory that there must have been *extraordinary* conditions – the psychological moment! There *must* have been a psychological moment when everyone's attention was mathematically centred elsewhere.'

'Our friend Inspector Japp is going to make minute inquiries on that point.'

'Do you not agree with me, M. Poirot?'

Poirot hesitated a minute, then he said slowly:

'I agree that there was – that there must have been a psychological reason why nobody saw the murderer . . . But my ideas are running in a slightly different channel from yours. I feel that in this case mere ocular facts may be deceptive. Close your eyes, my friend, instead of opening them wide. Use the eyes of the *brain*, not of the *body*. Let the little grey cells of the mind function . . . Let it be their task to show you *what actually happened*.'

Fournier stared at him curiously.

'I do not follow you, M. Poirot.'

'Because you are deducing from things that you have *seen*. Nothing can be so misleading as observation.'

Fournier shook his head again and spread out his hands. 'I give up. I cannot catch your meaning.'

'Our friend Giraud would urge you to pay no attention to my vagaries. "Be up and doing," he would say. "To sit still in an armchair and think, that is the method of an old man past his prime." But I say that a young hound is often so eager upon the scent that he overruns it . . . For him is the trail of the red herring. There, it is a very good hint I have given you there . . .'

And, leaning back, Poirot closed his eyes, it may have been to think, but it is quite certain that five minutes later he was fast asleep.

On arrival in Paris they went straight to No. 3 Rue Joliette.

The Rue Joliette is on the south side of the Seine. There

was nothing to distinguish No. 3 from the other houses. An aged concierge admitted them and greeted Fournier in a surly fashion.

'So we have the police here again! Nothing but trouble. This will give the house a bad name.'

He retreated grumbling into his apartment.

'We will go to Giselle's office,' said Fournier. 'It is on the first floor.'

He drew a key from his pocket as he spoke and explained that the French police had taken the precaution of locking and sealing the door whilst awaiting the result of the English inquest.

'Not, I fear,' said Fournier, 'that there is anything here to help us.'

He detached the seals, unlocked the door, and they entered. Madame Giselle's office was a small, stuffy apartment. It had a somewhat old-fashioned type of safe in a corner, a writing desk of business-like appearance and several shabbily upholstered chairs. The one window was dirty and it seemed highly probable that it had never been opened.

Fournier shrugged his shoulders as he looked round.

'You see?' he said. 'Nothing. Nothing at all.'

Poirot passed round behind the desk. He sat down in the chair and looked across the desk at Fournier. He passed his hand gently across the surface of the wood, then down underneath it.

'There is a bell here,' he said.

'Yes, it rings down to the concierge.'

'Ah, a wise precaution. Madame's clients might sometimes become obstreperous.'

He opened one or two of the drawers. They contained stationery, a calendar, pens and pencils, but no papers and nothing of a personal nature.

Poirot merely glanced into them in a cursory manner.

'I will not insult you, my friend, by a close search. If

there were anything to find you would have found it, I am sure.' He looked across at the safe. 'Not a very efficacious pattern, that?'

'Somewhat out of date,' agreed Fournier.

'It was empty?'

'Yes. That cursed maid had destroyed everything.'

'Ah, yes, the maid. The confidential maid. We must see her. This room, as you say, has nothing to tell us. It is significant that, do you not think so?'

'What do you mean by significant, M. Poirot?'

'I mean that there is in this room no personal touch . . . I find that interesting.'

'She was hardly a woman of sentiment,' said Fournier dryly.

Poirot rose.

'Come,' he said, 'let us see this maid – this highly confidential maid.'

Elise Grandier was a short stout woman of middle age with a florid face and small shrewd eyes that darted quickly from Fournier's face to that of his companion and then back again.

'Sit down, Mademoiselle Grandier,' said Fournier.

'Thank you, Monsieur.'

She sat down composedly.

'M. Poirot and I have returned today from London. The inquest – the inquiry, that is, into the death of Madame – took place yesterday. There is no doubt whatsoever. Madame was poisoned.'

The Frenchwoman shook her head gravely.

'It is terrible what you say there, Monsieur. Madame poisoned? Who would ever have dreamt of such a thing?'

'That is perhaps where you can help us, Mademoiselle.'

'Certainly, Monsieur, I will naturally do all I can to aid the police. But I know nothing – nothing at all.'

'You know that Madame had enemies?' said Fournier sharply.

86

'That is not true. Why should Madame have enemies?'

'Come, come, Mademoiselle Grandier,' said Fournier dryly. 'The profession of a moneylender – it entails certain unpleasantnesses.'

'It is true that sometimes the clients of Madame were not very reasonable,' agreed Elise.

'They made scenes, eh? They threatened her?'

The maid shook her head.

'No, no, you are wrong there. It was not *they* who threatened. They whined – they complained – they protested they could not pay – all that, yes.' Her voice held a very lively contempt.

'Sometimes, perhaps, Mademoiselle,' said Poirot, 'they could not pay.'

Elise Grandier shrugged her shoulders.

'Possibly. That is their affair! They usually paid in the end.'

Her tone held a certain amount of satisfaction.

'Madame Giselle was a hard woman,' said Fournier.

'Madame was justified.'

'You have no pity for the victims?'

'Victims – victims . . .' Elise spoke with impatience. 'You do not understand. Is it necessary to run into debt, to live beyond your means, to run and borrow, and then expect to keep the money as a gift? It is not reasonable, that! Madame was always fair and just. She lent – and she expected repayment. That is only fair. She herself had no debts. Always she paid honourably what she owed. Never, never were there any bills outstanding. And when you say that Madame was a hard woman it is not the truth! Madame was kind. She gave to the Little Sisters of the Poor when they came. She gave money to charitable institutions. When the wife of Georges, the concierge, was ill, Madame paid for her to go to a hospital in the country.'

She stopped, her face flushed and angry.

She repeated, 'You do not understand. No, you do not understand Madame at all.'

Fournier waited a moment for her indignation to subside and then said:

'You made the observation that Madame's clients usually managed to pay *in the end*. Were you aware of the means Madame used to compel them?'

She shrugged her shoulders.

'I know nothing, Monsieur – nothing at all.'

'You knew enough to burn Madame's papers.'

'I was following her instructions. If ever, she said, she were to meet with an accident, or if she were taken ill and died somewhere away from home, I was to destroy her business papers.'

'The papers in the safe downstairs?' asked Poirot.

'That is right. Her business papers.'

'And they were in the safe downstairs?'

His persistence brought the red up in Elise's cheeks.

'I obeyed Madame's instructions,' she said.

'I know that,' said Poirot, smiling. 'But the papers were not in the safe. That is so, is it not? That safe, it is far too old-fashioned – quite an amateur might have opened it. The papers were kept elsewhere – in Madame's bedroom, perhaps?'

Elise paused a moment and then answered:

'Yes, that is so. Madame always pretended to clients that papers were kept in the safe, but in reality the safe was a blind. Everything was in Madame's bedroom.'

'Will you show us where?'

Elise rose and the two men followed her. The bedroom was a fair-sized room, but was so full of ornate heavy furniture that it was hard to move about freely in it. In one corner was a large old-fashioned trunk. Elise lifted the lid and took out an old-fashioned alpaca dress with a silk underskirt. On the inside of the dress was a deep pocket.

'The papers were in this, Monsieur,' she said. 'They were kept in a large sealed envelope.'

'You told me nothing of this,' said Fournier sharply, 'when I questioned you three days ago.'

'I ask pardon, Monsieur. You asked me where were the papers that should be in the safe. I told you I had burned them. That was true. Exactly where the papers were kept seemed unimportant.'

'True,' said Fournier. 'You understand, Mademoiselle Grandier, that those papers should not have been burnt.'

'I obeyed Madame's orders,' said Elise sullenly.

'You acted, I know, for the best,' said Fournier soothingly. 'Now I want you to listen to me very closely, Mademoiselle: *Madame was murdered.* It is possible that she was murdered by a person or persons about whom she held certain damaging knowledge. That knowledge was in those papers you burnt. I am going to ask you a question, Mademoiselle, and do not reply too quickly without reflection. It is possible – *indeed in my view it is probable and quite understandable* – that you glanced through those papers before committing them to the flames. If that is the case, no blame will be attached to you for so doing. On the contrary, any information you have acquired may be of the greatest service to the police, and may be of material service in bringing the murderer to justice. Therefore, Mademoiselle, have no fear in answering truthfully. Did you, before burning the papers, glance over them?'

Elise breathed hard. She leant forward and spoke emphatically.

'No, Monsieur,' she said. 'I looked at nothing. I read nothing. I burnt the envelope without undoing the seal.'

CHAPTER 10

The Little Black Book

Fournier stared hard at her for a moment or two, then, satisfied that she was speaking the truth, he turned away with a gesture of discouragement.

'It is a pity,' he said. 'You acted honourably, Mademoiselle, but it is a pity.'

'I cannot help, Monsieur. I am sorry.'

Fournier sat down and drew a notebook from his pocket.

'When I questioned you before, you told me, Mademoiselle, that you did not know the names of Madame's clients. Yet just now you speak of them whining and asking for mercy. You did, therefore, know *something* about these clients of Madame Giselle's?'

'Let me explain, Monsieur. Madame never mentioned a name. She never discussed her business. But all the same one is human, is one not? There are ejaculations – comments. Madame spoke to me sometimes as she would to herself.'

Poirot leaned forward.

'If you would give us an instance, Mademoiselle –' he said.

'Let me see – ah, yes – say a letter comes. Madame opens it. She laughs a short, dry laugh. She says, "*You whine and you snivel, my fine lady. All the same, you must pay.*" Or she would say to me, "*What fools! What fools! To think I would lend large sums without proper security. Knowledge is security, Elise. Knowledge is power.*" Something like that she would say.'

'Madame's clients who came to the house, did you ever see any of them?'

'No, Monsieur – at least hardly ever. They came to the

first floor only, you understand, and very often they came after dark.'

'Had Madame Giselle been in Paris before her journey to England?'

'She returned to Paris only the afternoon before.'

'Where had she been?'

'She had been away for a fortnight to Deauville, Le Pinet, Paris-Plage and Wimereux – her usual September round.'

'Now think, Mademoiselle, did she say *anything* – anything at all that might be of use?'

Elise considered for some moments. Then she shook her head.

'No, Monsieur,' she said. 'I cannot remember anything. Madame was in good spirits. Business was going well, she said. Her tour had been profitable. Then she directed me to ring up Universal Airlines and book a passage to England for the following day. The early morning service was booked, but she obtained a seat on the 12 o'clock service.'

'Did she say what took her to England? Was there any urgency about it?'

'Oh, no, Monsieur. Madame journeyed to England fairly frequently. She usually told me the day before.'

'Did any clients come to see Madame that evening?'

'I believe there was one client, Monsieur, but I am not sure. Georges, perhaps, would know. Madame said nothing to me.'

Fournier took from his pockets various photographs – mostly snapshots taken by reporters, of various witnesses leaving the coroner's court.

'Can you recognize any of these, Mademoiselle?'

Elise took them and gazed at each in turn. Then she shook her head.

'No, Monsieur.'

'We must try Georges then.'

'Yes, Monsieur. Unfortunately, Georges has not very good eyesight. It is a pity.'

91

Fournier rose.

'Well Mademoiselle, we will take our leave – that is, if you are quite sure that there is nothing – nothing at all – that you have omitted to mention.'

'I? What – what could there be?'

Elise looked distressed.

'It is understood, then. Come, M. Poirot. I beg your pardon. You are looking for something?'

Poirot was indeed wandering round the room in a vague searching way.

'It is true,' said Poirot. 'I am looking for something I do not see.'

'What is that?'

'Photographs. Photographs of Madame Giselle's relations – of her family.'

Elise shook her head.

'She had no family, Madame. She was alone in the world.'

'She had a daughter,' said Poirot sharply.

'Yes, that is so. Yes, she had a daughter.'

Elise sighed.

'But there is no picture of that daughter?' Poirot persisted.

'Oh, Monsieur does not understand. It is true that Madame had a daughter, but that was long ago, you comprehend. It is my belief that Madame had never seen that daughter since she was a tiny baby.'

'How was that?' demanded Fournier sharply.

Elise's hands flew out in an expressive gesture.

'I do not know. It was in the days when Madame was young. I have heard that she was pretty then – pretty and poor. She may have been married; she may not. Myself, I think not. Doubtless some arrangement was made about the child. As for Madame, she had the smallpox – she was very ill – she nearly died. When she got well her beauty was gone. There were no more follies, no more romance. Madame became a woman of business.'

'But she left her money to this daughter?'

'That is only right,' said Elise. 'Who should one leave one's money to except one's own flesh and blood? Blood is thicker than water; and Madame had no friends. She was always alone. Money was her passion – to make more and more money. She spent very little. She had no love for luxury.'

'She left you a legacy. You know that?'

'But yes, I have been informed. Madame was always generous. She gave me a good sum every year as well as my wages. I am very grateful to Madame.'

'Well,' said Fournier, 'we will take our leave. On the way out I will have another word with old Georges.'

'Permit me to follow you in a little minute, my friend,' said Poirot.

'As you wish.'

Fournier departed.

Poirot roamed once more round the room, then sat down and fixed his eyes on Elise.

Under his scrutiny the Frenchwoman got slightly restive.

'Is there anything more Monsieur requires to know?'

'Mademoiselle Grandier,' said Poirot, 'do you know who murdered your mistress?'

'No, Monsieur. Before the good God I swear it.'

She spoke very earnestly. Poirot looked at her searchingly, then bent his head.

'*Bien*,' he said. 'I accept that. But knowledge is one thing, suspicion is another. Have you any idea – an *idea* only – who might have done such a thing?'

'I have no idea, Monsieur. I have already said so to the agent of police.'

'You might say one thing to him and another thing to me.'

'Why do you say that, Monsieur? Why should I do such a thing?'

'Because it is one thing to give information to the police and another thing to give it to a private individual.'

'Yes,' admitted Elise. 'That is true.'

A look of indecision came over her face. She seemed to be thinking. Watching her very closely, Poirot leaned forward and spoke:

'Shall I tell you something, Mademoiselle Grandier? It is part of my business to believe nothing I am told – nothing that is, that is not *proved*. I do not suspect first this person and then that person. I suspect *everybody*. Anybody connected with a crime is regarded by me as a criminal until that person is proved innocent.'

Elise Grandier scowled at him angrily.

'Are you saying that you suspect me – *me* – of having murdered Madame? It is too strong, that! Such a thought is of a wickedness unbelievable!'

Her large bosom rose and fell tumultuously.

'No, Elise,' said Poirot. 'I do not suspect you of having murdered Madame. Whoever murdered Madame was a passenger in the aeroplane. Therefore it was not your hand that did the deed. But you might have been *an accomplice before the act*. You might have passed on to someone the details of Madame's journey.'

'I did not. I swear I did not.'

Poirot looked at her again for some minutes in silence. Then he nodded his head.

'I believe you,' he said. 'But, nevertheless, there is something that you conceal. Oh, yes there is! Listen, I will tell you something. In every case of a criminal nature one comes across the same phenomena when questioning witnesses. *Everyone keeps something back*. Sometimes – often indeed – it is something quite harmless, something, perhaps, quite unconnected with the crime; but – I say it again – there is always *something*. That is so with you. Oh, do not deny! I am Hercule Poirot and I *know*. When my friend M. Fournier asked you if you were sure there was nothing you had omitted to mention, you were troubled. You answered unconsciously, with an evasion. Again just now when I

94

suggested that you might tell me something which you would not care to tell the police you very obviously turned the suggestion over in your mind. There is, then, *something*. I want to know what that something is.'

'It is nothing of importance.'

'Possibly not. But all the same, will you not tell me what it is? Remember,' he went on as she hesitated, 'I am not of the police.'

'That is true,' said Elise Grandier. She hesitated and went on, 'Monsieur, I am in a difficulty. I do not know what Madame herself would have wanted me to do.'

'There is a saying that two heads are better than one. Will you not consult me? Let us examine the question together.'

The woman still looked at him doubtfully. He said with a smile:

'You are a good watch-dog Elise. It is a question, I see, of loyalty to your dead mistress?'

'That is quite right, Monsieur. Madame trusted me. Ever since I entered her service I have carried out her instructions faithfully.'

'You were grateful, were you not, for some great service she had rendered you?'

'Monsieur is very quick. Yes, that is true. I do not mind admitting it. I had been deceived, Monsieur, my savings stolen – and there was a child. Madame was good to me. She arranged for the baby to be brought up by some good people on a farm – a good farm, Monsieur, and honest people. It was then, at that time, that she mentioned to me that she, too, was a mother.'

'Did she tell you the age of her child, where it was, any details?'

'No, Monsieur, she spoke of a part of her life that was over and done with. It was best so, she said. The little girl was well provided for and would be brought up to a trade or profession. She would also inherit her money when she died.'

'She told you nothing further about this child or about its father?'

'No, Monsieur, but I have an idea –'

'Speak, Mademoiselle Elise.'

'It is an idea only, you understand.'

'Perfectly, perfectly.'

'I have an idea that the father of the child was an Englishman.'

'What exactly do you think gave you that impression?'

'Nothing definite. It is just that there was a bitterness in Madame's voice when she spoke of the English. I think, too, that in her business transactions she enjoyed having anyone English in her power. It is an impression only –'

'Yes, but it may be a very valuable one. It opens up possibilities . . . Your own child, Mademoiselle Elise? Was it a girl or a boy?'

'A girl, Monsieur. But she is dead – dead these five years now.'

'Ah – all my sympathy.'

There was a pause.

'And now, Mademoiselle Elise,' said Poirot, 'what is this something that you have hitherto refrained from mentioning?'

Elise rose and left the room. She returned a few minutes later with a small shabby black notebook in her hand.

'This little book was Madame's. It went with her everywhere. When she was about to depart for England she could not find it. It was mislaid. After she had gone I found it. It had dropped down behind the head of the bed. I put it in my room to keep until Madame should return. I burned the papers as soon as I heard of Madame's death, but I did not burn the book. There were no instructions as to that.'

'When did you hear of Madame's death?'

Elise hesitated a minute.

'You heard it from the police, did you not?' said Poirot. 'They came here and examined Madame's rooms. They

96

found the safe empty and you told them that you had burnt the papers, but actually you did not burn the papers until afterwards.'

'It is true, Monsieur,' admitted Elise. 'Whilst they were looking in the safe I removed the papers from the trunk. I said they were burnt, yes. After all, it was very nearly the truth. I burnt them at the first opportunity. I had to carry out Madame's orders. You see my difficulty, Monsieur? You will not inform the police? It might be a very serious matter for me.'

'I believe, Mademoiselle Elise, that you acted with the best intentions. All the same, you understand, it is a pity . . . a great pity. But it does no good to regret what is done, and I see no necessity for communicating the exact hour of the destruction to the excellent M. Fournier. Now let me see if there is anything in this little book to aid us.'

'I do not think there will be, Monsieur,' said Elise, shaking her head. 'It is Madame's private memorandums, yes, but there are numbers only. Without the documents and files these entries are meaningless.'

Unwillingly she held out the book to Poirot. He took it and turned the pages. There were pencilled entries in a sloping foreign writing. They seemed to be all of the same kind. A number followed by a few descriptive details, such as:

CX 256. Colonel's wife. Stationed Syria. Regimental funds.
GF 342. French Deputy. Stavisky connexion.

The entries seemed to be all of the same kind. There were perhaps twenty in all. At the end of the book were pencilled memoranda of dates or places, such as:

Le Pinet, Monday. Casino, 10.30. Savoy Hotel, 5 o'clock.
ABC. Fleet Street, 11 o'clock.

None of these were complete in themselves, and seemed to have been put down less as actual appointments than as aids to Giselle's memory.

Elise was watching Poirot anxiously.

97

'It means nothing, Monsieur, or so it seems to me. It was comprehensible to Madame, but not to a mere reader.'

Poirot closed the book and put it in his pocket.

'This may be very valuable, Mademoiselle. You did wisely to give it to me. And your conscience may be quite at rest. Madame never asked you to burn this book?'

'That is true,' said Elise, her face brightening a little.

'Therefore, having no instructions, it is your duty to hand this over to the police. I will arrange matters with M. Fournier so that you shall not be blamed for not having done so sooner.'

'Monsieur is very kind.'

Poirot rose.

'I will go now and join my colleague. Just one last question. When you reserved a seat in the aeroplane for Madame Giselle, did you ring up the aerodrome at Le Bourget or the office of the company?'

'I rang up the office of Universal Airlines, Monsieur.'

'And that, I think, is in the Boulevard des Capucines?'

'That is right, Monsieur, 254 Boulevard des Capucines.'

Poirot inscribed the number in his little book, then with a friendly nod he left the room.

CHAPTER 11

The American

Fournier was deep in conversation with old Georges. The detective was looking hot and annoyed.

'Just like the police,' the old man was grumbling in his deep hoarse voice. 'Ask one the same question over and over again. What do they hope for? That sooner or later one will give over speaking the truth and take to lies instead? Agreeable lies, naturally, lies that suit the book of *ces Messieurs*.'

'It is not lies I want, but the truth.'

'Very well, it is the truth that I have been telling you. Yes, a woman did come to see Madame the night before she left for England. You show me those photographs, you ask me if I recognize the woman among them. I tell you what I have told you all along – my present eyesight is not good – it was growing dark – I did not look closely. I did not recognize the lady. If I saw her face to face I should probably not recognize her. There! You have it plainly for the fourth or fifth time.'

'And you cannot even remember if she was tall or short, dark or fair, young or old? It is hardly to be believed, that.'

Fournier spoke with irritable sarcasm.

'Then do not believe it. What do I care? A nice thing – to be mixed up with the police! I am ashamed. If Madame had not been killed high up in the air you would probably pretend that I, Georges, had poisoned her. The police are like that.'

Poirot forestalled an angry retort on Fournier's part by slipping a tactful arm through that of his friend.

'Come, *mon vieux*,' he said. 'The stomach calls. A simple but satisfying meal, that is what I prescribe. Let us say *omelette aux champignons, sole à la Normande* – a cheese of Port Salut, and with it red wine. What wine exactly?'

Fournier glanced at his watch.

'True,' he said. 'It is one o'clock. Talking to this animal here –' He glared at Georges.

Poirot smiled encouragingly at the old man.

'It is understood,' he said. 'The nameless lady was neither tall nor short, fair nor dark, thin nor fat, but this at least you can tell us: Was she chic?'

'Chic?' said Georges, rather taken aback.

'I am answered,' said Poirot. 'She was *chic*. And I have a little idea, my friend, that she would look well in a bathing-dress.'

Georges stared at him.

'A bathing-dress? What is this about a bathing-dress?'

'A little idea of mine. A charming woman looks still more charming in a bathing-dress. Do you not agree? See here.'

He passed to the old man a page torn from the *Sketch*.

There was a moment's pause. The old man gave a very slight start.

'You agree, do you not?' asked Poirot.

'They look well enough, those two,' said the old man, handing the sheet back. 'To wear nothing at all would be very nearly the same thing.'

'Ah,' said Poirot. 'That is because nowadays we have discovered the beneficial action of sun on the skin. It is very convenient, that.'

Georges condescended to give a hoarse chuckle, and moved away as Poirot and Fournier stepped out into the sunlit street.

Over the meal as outlined by Poirot, the little Belgian produced the little black memorandum book.

Fournier was much excited, though distinctly irate with Elise. Poirot argued the point.

'It is natural – very natural. The police? It is always a word frightening to that class. It embroils them in they know not what. It is the same everywhere – in every country.'

'That is where *you* score,' said Fournier. 'The private investigator gets more out of witnesses than you ever get through official channels. However, there is the other side of the picture. We have official records – the whole system of a big organization at our command.'

'So let us work together amicably,' said Poirot, smiling. 'This omelette is delicious.'

In the interval between the omelette and the sole, Fournier turned the pages of the black book. Then he made a pencilled entry in his notebook.

He looked across at Poirot.

'You have read through this? Yes?'

'No. I have only glanced at it. You permit?'

He took the book from Fournier.

When the cheese was placed before them Poirot laid down the book on the table, and the eyes of the two men met.

'There are certain entries,' began Fournier.

'Five,' said Poirot.

'I agree – five.'

He read out from his pocket-book:

'*CL 52. English Peeress. Husband.*
RT 362. Doctor. Harley Street.
MR 24. Forged Antiquities.
XVB 724. English. Embezzlement.
GF 45. Attempted Murder. English.'

'Excellent, my friend,' said Poirot. 'Our minds march together to a marvel. Of all the entries in that little book, those five seem to me to be the only ones that can in any way bear a relation to the persons travelling in the aeroplane. Let us take them one by one.'

'*English Peeress. Husband*,' said Fournier. 'That may conceivably apply to Lady Horbury. She is, I understand, a confirmed gambler. Nothing could be more likely than that she should borrow money from Giselle. Giselle's clients are usually of that type. The word *husband* may have one of two

101

meanings. Either Giselle expected the husband to pay up his wife's debts, or she had some hold over Lady Horbury, a secret which she threatened to reveal to the lady's husband.'

'Precisely,' said Poirot. 'Either of those two alternatives might apply. I favour the second one myself, especially as I would be prepared to bet that the woman who visited Giselle the night before the aeroplane journey was Lady Horbury.'

'Ah, you think that, do you?'

'Yes, and I fancy you think the same. There is a touch of chivalry, I think, in our *concierge's* disposition. His persistence in remembering nothing at all about the visitor seems rather significant. Lady Horbury is an extremely pretty woman. Moreover, I observed his start – oh, a very slight one – when I handed him a reproduction of her in bathing costume from the *Sketch*. Yes, it was Lady Horbury who went to Giselle's that night.'

'She followed her to Paris from Le Pinet,' said Fournier slowly. 'It looks as though she were pretty desperate.'

'Yes, yes, I fancy that may be true.'

Fournier looked at him curiously.

'But it does not square with your private ideas, eh?'

'My friend, as I tell you, I have what I am convinced is the right clue pointing to the wrong person. . . . I am very much in the dark. My clue cannot be wrong; and yet –'

'You wouldn't like to tell me what it is?' suggested Fournier.

'No, because I may, you see, be wrong – totally and utterly wrong. And in that case I might lead you, too, astray. No, let us each work according to our own ideas. To continue with our selected items from the little book.'

'*RT 362. Doctor. Harley Street*,' read out Fournier.

'A possible clue to Dr Bryant. There is nothing much to go on, but we must not neglect that line of investigation.'

'That, of course, will be the task of Inspector Japp.'

'And mine,' said Poirot. 'I, too, have my finger in this pie.'

'*MR 24. Forged Antiquities*,' read Fournier. 'Far fetched, perhaps, but it is just possible that that might apply to the Duponts. I can hardly credit it. M. Dupont is an archaeologist of world-wide reputation. He bears the highest character.'

'Which would facilitate matters very much for him,' said Poirot. 'Consider, my dear Fournier, how high has been the character, how lofty the sentiments, and how worthy of admiration the life of most swindlers of note – *before they are found out*!'

'True, only too true,' agreed the Frenchman with a sigh.

'A high reputation,' said Poirot, 'is the first necessity of a swindler's stock in trade. An interesting thought. But let us return to our list.'

'*XVB 724* is very ambiguous. *English. Embezzlement.*'

'Not very helpful,' agreed Poirot. 'Who embezzles? A solicitor? A bank clerk? Anyone in a position of trust in a commercial firm. Hardly an author, a dentist or a doctor. Mr James Ryder is the only representative of commerce. He may have embezzled money, he may have borrowed from Giselle to enable his theft to remain undetected. As to the last entry – *GF 45. Attempted Murder. English* – that gives us a very wide field. Author, dentist, doctor, business man, steward, hairdresser's assistant, lady of birth and breeding – any one of those might be *GF 45*. In fact only the Duponts are exempt by reason of their nationality.'

With a gesture he summoned the waiter and asked for the bill.

'And where next, my friend?' he inquired.

'To the Sûreté. They may have some news for me.'

'Good. I will accompany you. Afterwards I have a little investigation of my own to make in which, perhaps, you will assist me.'

At the Sûreté Poirot renewed acquaintance with the Chief of the Detective Force, whom he had met some years previously in the course of one of his cases. M. Gilles was very affable and polite.

'Enchanted to learn that you are interesting yourself in this case, M. Poirot.'

'My faith, my dear M. Gilles, it happened under my nose. It is an insult, that, you agree? Hercule Poirot to sleep while murder is committed!'

M. Gilles shook his head tactfully.

'These machines! On a day of bad weather they are far from steady, far from steady. I myself have felt seriously incommoded once or twice.'

'They say that an army marches on its stomach,' said Poirot. 'But how much are the delicate convolutions of the brain influenced by the digestive apparatus? When the *mal de mer* seizes me I, Hercule Poirot, am a creature with no grey cells, no order, no method – a mere member of the human race somewhat below average intelligence! It is deplorable, but there it is! And talking of these matters, how is my excellent friend Giraud?'

Prudently ignoring the significance of the words 'these matters', M. Gilles replied that Giraud continued to advance in his career.

'He is most zealous. His energy is untiring.'

'It always was,' said Poirot. 'He ran to and fro. He crawled on all fours. He was here, there and everywhere. Not for one moment did he ever pause and reflect.'

'Ah, M. Poirot, that is your little foible. A man like Fournier will be more to your mind. He is of the newest school – all for the psychology. That should please you.'

'It does. It does.'

'He has a very good knowledge of English. That is why we sent him to Croydon to assist in this case. A very interesting case, M. Poirot. Madame Giselle was one of the best-known characters in Paris. And the manner of her death – extraordinary! A poisoned dart from a blowpipe in an aeroplane. I ask you! Is it possible that such a thing could happen?'

'Exactly,' cried Poirot. 'Exactly. You hit the nail upon

the head. You place a finger unerringly – Ah, here is our good Fournier. You have news, I see.'

The melancholy-faced Fournier was looking quite eager and excited.

'Yes, indeed. A Greek antique dealer, Zeropoulos, has reported the sale of a blowpipe and darts three days before the murder. I propose now, Monsieur' – he bowed respectfully to his chief – 'to interview this man.'

'By all means,' said Gilles. 'Does M. Poirot accompany you?'

'If you please,' said Poirot. 'This is interesting – very interesting.'

The shop of M. Zeropoulos was in the Rue St Honoré. It was by way of being a high-class antique dealer's. There was a good deal of Rhages ware and other Persian pottery. There were one or two bronzes from Louristan, a good deal of inferior Indian jewellery, shelves of silks and embroideries from many countries, and a large proportion of perfectly worthless beads and cheap Egyptian goods. It was the kind of establishment in which you could spend a million francs on an object worth half a million, or ten francs on an object worth fifty centimes. It was patronized chiefly by American tourists and knowledgeable connoisseurs.

M. Zeropoulos himself was a short, stout little man with beady black eyes. He talked volubly and at great length.

The gentlemen were from the police? He was delighted to see them. Perhaps they would step into his private office. Yes, he had sold a blowpipe and darts – a South American curio – 'you comprehend, gentlemen, me, I sell a little of everything! I have my specialities. Persia is my speciality. M. Dupont, the esteemed M. Dupont he will answer for me. He himself comes always to see my collection – to see what new purchases I have made – to give his judgement on the genuineness of certain doubtful pieces. What a man! So learned! Such an eye! Such a *feel*. But I wander from the point. I have my collection – my valuable collection that all

105

connoisseurs know – and also I have – well, frankly, Messieurs, let us call it junk! Foreign junk, that is understood, a little bit of everything – from the South Seas, from India, from Japan, from Borneo. No matter! Usually I have no fixed price for these things. If anyone takes an interest I make my estimate and I ask a price, and naturally I am beaten down, and in the end I take only half. And even then, I will admit it, the profit is good! These articles, I buy them from sailors usually at a very low price.'

M. Zeropoulos took a breath and went on happily, delighted with himself, his importance and the easy flow of his narration.

'This blowpipe and darts I have had it for a long time – two years, perhaps. It was in that tray there, with a cowrie necklace and a Red Indian headdress, and one or two crude wooden idols and some inferior jade beads. Nobody remarks it, nobody notices it till there comes this American and asks me what it is.'

'An American?' said Fournier sharply.

'Yes, yes, an American – unmistakably an American. Not the best type of American, either – the kind that knows nothing about anything and just wants a curio to take home. He is of the type that makes the fortune of bead sellers in Egypt – that buys the most preposterous scarabs ever made in Czecho-Slovakia. Well, very quickly I size him up, I tell him about the habits of certain tribes, the deadly poisons they use. I explain how very rare and unusual it is that anything of this kind comes into the market. He asks the price and I tell him. It is my American price, not quite as high as formerly (alas! they have had the depression over there). I wait for him to bargain, but straightaway he pays my price. I am stupefied. It is a pity; I might have asked more! I give him the blowpipe and the darts wrapped up in a parcel and he takes them away. It is finished. But afterwards when I read in the paper of this astounding murder I wonder – yes, I wonder very much. And I communicate with the police.'

'We are much obliged to you, M. Zeropoulos,' said Fournier politely. 'This blowpipe and dart – you think you would be able to identify them? At the moment they are in London, you understand, but an opportunity will be given you of identifying them.'

'The blowpipe was about so long,' M. Zeropoulos measured a space on his desk, 'and so thick – you see, like this pen of mine. It was of a light colour. There were four darts. They were long pointed thorns, slightly discoloured at the tips, with a little fluff of red silk on them.'

'*Red silk*?' asked Poirot keenly.

'Yes, Monsieur. A cerise red – somewhat faded.'

'That is curious,' said Fournier. 'You are sure that there was not one of them with a black and yellow fluff of silk?'

'Black and yellow? No, Monsieur.'

The dealer shook his head.

Fournier glanced at Poirot. There was a curious satisfied smile on the little man's face.

Fournier wondered why. Was it because Zeropoulos was lying, or was it for some other reason?

Fournier said doubtfully, 'It is very possible that this blowpipe and dart has nothing whatever to do with the case. It is just one chance in fifty, perhaps. Nevertheless, I should like as full a description as possible of this American.'

Zeropoulos spread out a pair of Oriental hands.

'He was just an American. His voice was in his nose. He could not speak French. He was chewing the gum. He had tortoise-shell glasses. He was tall and, I think, not very old.'

'Fair or dark?'

'I could hardly say. He had his hat on.'

'Would you know him again if you saw him?'

Zeropoulos seemed doubtful.

'I could not say. So many Americans come and go. He was not remarkable in any way.'

Fournier showed him the collection of snapshots, but without avail. None of them, Zeropoulos thought, was the man.

107

'Probably a wild-goose chase,' said Fournier as they left the shop.

'It is possible, yes,' agreed Poirot. 'But I do not think so. The price tickets were of the same shape and there are one or two points of interest about the story and about M. Zeropoulos's remarks. And now, my friend, having been upon one wild-goose chase, indulge me and come upon another.'

'Where to?'

'To the Boulevard des Capucines.'

'Let me see, that is –?'

'The office of Universal Airlines.'

'Of course. But we have already made perfunctory inquiries there. They could tell us nothing of interest.'

Poirot tapped him kindly on the shoulder.

'Ah, but, you see, an answer depends on the questions. You did not know what questions to ask.'

'And you do?'

'Well, I have a certain little idea.'

He would say no more, and in due course they arrived at the Boulevard des Capucines.

The office of Universal Airlines was quite small. A smart-looking dark man was behind a highly-polished wooden counter and a boy of about fifteen was sitting at a typewriter.

Fournier produced his credentials and the man, whose name was Jules Perrot, declared himself to be entirely at their service.

At Poirot's suggestion, the typewriting boy was dispatched to the farthest corner.

'It is very confidential what we have to say,' he explained.

Jules Perrot looked pleasantly excited.

'Yes, Messieurs?'

'It is this matter of the murder of Madame Giselle.'

'Ah, yes, I recollect. I think I have already answered some questions on the subject.'

'Precisely, precisely. But it is necessary to have the facts very exactly. Now Madame Giselle received her place – when?'

'I think that point has already been settled. She booked her seat by telephone on the 17th.'

'That was for the 12 o'clock service on the following day?'

'Yes, Monsieur.'

'But I understand from her maid that it was on the 8.45 am service that Madame reserved a seat.'

'No, no – at least this is what happened. Madame's maid asked for the 8.45 service, but that service was already booked up, so we gave her a seat on the 12 o'clock instead.'

'Ah, I see. I see.'

'Yes, Monsieur.'

'I see – I see – but all the same it is curious – decidedly it is curious.'

The clerk looked at him inquiringly.

'It is only that a friend of mine decided to go to England at a moment's notice, went to England on the 8.45 service that morning, and the plane was half empty.'

M. Perrot turned over some papers. He blew his nose.

'Possibly your friend has mistaken the day. The day before or the day after –'

'Not at all. It was the day of the murder, because my friend said that if he had missed the plane, as he nearly did, he would have actually been one of the passengers in the *Prometheus*.'

'Ah, indeed. Yes, very curious. Of course, sometimes people do not arrive at the last minute, and then, naturally, there are vacant places . . . and then sometimes there are mistakes. I have to get in touch with Le Bourget; they are not always accurate –'

The mild inquiring gaze of Hercule Poirot seemed to be upsetting to Jules Perrot. He came to a stop. His eyes shifted. A little bead of perspiration came out on his forehead.

'Two quite possible explanations,' said Poirot, 'but somehow, I fancy, not the true explanation. Don't you think it might perhaps be better to make a clean breast of the matter?'

'A clean breast of what? I don't understand you.'

'Come, come. You understand me very well. This is a case of murder – *murder*, M. Perrot. Remember that, if you please. If you withhold information it may well be very serious for you – very serious indeed. The police will take a very grave view. You are obstructing the ends of justice.'

Jules Perrot stared at him. His mouth fell open. His hands shook.

'Come,' said Poirot. His voice was authoritative, autocratic. 'We want precise information, if you please. How much were you paid, and who paid you?'

'I meant no harm – I had no idea – I never guessed . . .'

'How much, and who by?'

'F-five thousand francs. I never saw the man before. I – this will ruin me . . .'

'What will ruin you is not to speak out. Come, now, we know the worst. Tell us exactly how it happened.'

The perspiration rolling down his forehead, Jules Perrot spoke rapidly in little jerks.

'I meant no harm . . . Upon my honour, I meant no harm. A man came in. He said he was going to England on the following day. He wanted to negotiate a loan from – from Madame Giselle, but he wanted their meeting to be unpremeditated. He said it would give him a better chance. He said that he knew she was going to England on the following day. All I had to do was to tell her the early service was full up and to give her seat No. 2 in the *Prometheus*. I swear, Messieurs, that I saw nothing very wrong in that. What difference could it make? – that is what I thought. Americans are like that – they do business in unconventional ways –'

'Americans?' said Fournier sharply.

'Yes, this Monsieur was an American.'

'Describe him.'

'He was tall, stooped, had grey hair, horn-rimmed glasses and a little goatee beard.'

'Did he book a seat himself?'

'Yes, Monsieur, seat No. 1 – next to – to the one I was to keep for Madame Giselle.'

'In what name?'

'Silas – Silas Harper.'

'There was no one of that name travelling, and no one occupied seat No. 1.'

Poirot shook his head gently.

'I saw by the paper that there was no one of that name. That is why I thought there was no need to mention the matter. Since this man did not go by the plane –'

Fournier shot him a cold glance.

'You have withheld valuable information from the police,' he said. 'This is a very serious matter.'

Together he and Poirot left the office, leaving Jules Perrot staring after them with a frightened face.

On the pavement outside, Fournier removed his hat and bowed.

'I salute you, M. Poirot. What gave you this idea?'

'Two separate sentences. One this morning when I heard a man in our plane say that he had crossed on the morning of the murder in a nearly empty plane. The second sentence was that uttered by Elise when she said that she rung up the office of Universal Airlines and that there was no room on the early morning service. Now those two statements did not agree. I remembered the steward on the *Prometheus* saying that he had seen Madame Giselle before on the early service – so it was clearly her custom to go by the 8.45 am plane.

'*But somebody wanted her to go on the 12 o'clock* – somebody was already travelling by the *Prometheus*. Why did the clerk say that the early service was booked up? A

111

mistake, or a deliberate lie? I fancied the latter . . . I was right.'

'Every minute this case gets more puzzling,' cried Fournier. 'First we seem to be on the track of a woman. Now it is a man. This American –'

He stopped and looked at Poirot.

The latter nodded gently.

'Yes, my friend,' he said. 'It is so easy to be an American – here in Paris! A nasal voice – the chewing gum – the little goatee – the horn-rimmed spectacles – all the appurtenances of the stage American . . .'

He took from his pocket the page he had torn from the *Sketch*.

'What are you looking at?'

'At a Countess in her bathing suit.'

'You think –? But no, she is petite, charming, fragile – she could not impersonate a tall stooping American. She has been an actress, yes, but to act such a part is out of the question. No, my friend, that idea will not do.'

'I never said it would,' said Hercule Poirot.

And still he looked earnestly at the printed page.

CHAPTER 12

At Horbury Chase

Lord Horbury stood by the sideboard and helped himself absent-mindedly to kidneys.

Stephen Horbury was twenty-seven years of age. He had a narrow head and a long chin. He looked very much what he was – a sporting out-of-door kind of man without anything very spectacular in the way of brains. He was kind-hearted, slightly priggish, intensely loyal and invincibly obstinate.

He took his heaped plate back to the table and began to eat. Presently he opened a newspaper, but immediately, with a frown, he cast it aside. He thrust aside his unfinished plate, drank some coffee and rose to his feet. He paused uncertainly for a minute, then with a slight nod of the head he left the dining-room, crossed the wide hall and went upstairs. He tapped at a door and waited for a minute. From inside the room a clear high voice cried out, 'Come in.'

Lord Horbury went in.

It was a wide beautiful bedroom facing south. Cicely Horbury was in bed, a great carved oak Elizabethan bed. Very lovely she looked, too, in her rose chiffon draperies, with the curling gold of her hair. A breakfast tray with the remains of orange juice and coffee on it was on a table beside her. She was opening her letters. Her maid was moving about the room.

Any man might be excused if his breath came a little faster confronted by so much loveliness; but the charming picture his wife presented affected Lord Horbury not at all.

There had been a time, three years ago, when the breathtaking loveliness of his Cicely had set the young man's senses reeling. He had been madly, wildly, passionately in love. All that was over. He had been mad. He was now sane.

Lady Horbury said in some surprise:

'Why, Stephen?'

He said abruptly, 'I'd like to talk to you alone.'

'Madeleine.' Lady Horbury spoke to her maid. 'Leave all that. Get out.'

The French girl murmured, '*Très bien*, M'lady', shot a quick interested look out of the corner of her eye at Lord Horbury and left the room.

Lord Horbury waited till she had shut the door, then he said:

'I'd like to know, Cicely, just exactly what is behind this idea of coming down here.'

Lady Horbury shrugged her slender, beautiful shoulders.

'After all, why not?'

'Why not? It seems to me there are a good many reasons.'

His wife murmured, 'Oh, reasons . . .'

'Yes, reasons. You'll remember that we agreed that as things were between us, it would be as well to give up this farce of living together. You were to have the town house and a generous – an extremely generous – allowance. Within certain limits you were to go your own way. Why this sudden return?'

Again Cicely shrugged her shoulders.

'I thought it – better.'

'You mean, I suppose, that it's money?'

Lady Horbury said, 'My God, how I hate you. You're the meanest man alive.'

'Mean? Mean, you say, when it's because of you and your senseless extravagance that there's a mortgage on Horbury.'

'Horbury – Horbury – that's all you care for! Horses and hunting and shooting and crops and tiresome old farmers. God, what a life for a woman.'

'Some women enjoy it.'

'Yes, women like Venetia Kerr, who's half a horse herself. You ought to have married a woman like that.'

Lord Horbury walked over the the window.

'It's a little late to say that. I married you.'

'And you can't get out of it,' said Cicely. Her laugh was malicious, triumphant. 'You'd like to get rid of me, but you can't.'

He said, 'Need we go into all this?'

'Very much God and the Old School, aren't you? Most of my friends fairly laugh their heads off when I tell them the kind of things you say.'

'They are welcome to do so. Shall we get back to our original subject of discussion – your reason for coming here?'

But his wife would not follow his lead. She said:

'You advertised in the papers that you wouldn't be responsible for my debts. Do you call that a gentlemanly thing to do?'

'I regret having had to take that step. I warned you, you will remember. Twice I paid up. But there are limits. Your insensate passion for gambling – well, why discuss it? But I do want to know what prompted you to come down to Horbury. You've always hated the place, been bored to death here.'

Cicely Horbury, her small face sullen, said, 'I thought it better – just now.'

'Better – just now?' He repeated the words thoughtfully. Then he asked a question sharply: 'Cicely, had you been borrowing from that old French moneylender?'

'Which one? I don't know what you mean.'

'You know perfectly what I mean. I mean the woman who was murdered on the plane from Paris – the plane on which you travelled home. Had you borrowed money from her?'

'No, of course not. What an idea!'

'Now, don't be a little fool over this, Cicely. If that woman did lend you money, you'd better tell me about it. Remember the business isn't over and finished with. The verdict at the inquest was wilful murder by a person or persons unknown. The police of both countries are at work. It's only a matter of time before they come on the truth. The woman's sure to have left records of her dealings. If anything crops up to connect you with her we should be prepared beforehand. We must have ffoulkes's advice on the matter.' (ffoulkes, ffoulkes, Wilbraham and ffoulkes were the family solicitors who for generations had dealt with the Horbury estate.)

'Didn't I give evidence in that damned court and say I had never heard of the woman?'

'I don't think that proves very much,' said her husband dryly. 'If you did have dealings with this Giselle, you can be sure the police will find it out.'

Cicely sat up angrily in bed.

'Perhaps you think I killed her – stood up there in that plane and puffed darts at her from a blowpipe. Of all the crazy businesses!'

'The whole thing sounds mad,' Stephen agreed thoughtfully. 'But I do want you to realize your position.'

'What position? There isn't any position. You don't believe a word I say. It's damnable. And why be so anxious about me all of a sudden? A lot you care about what happens to me. You dislike me. You hate me. You'd be glad if I died tomorrow. Why pretend?'

'Aren't you exaggerating a little? In any case, old-fashioned though you think me, I do happen to care about my family name – an out-of-date sentiment which you will probably despise. But there it is.'

Turning abruptly on his heel, he left the room.

A pulse was beating in his temple. Thoughts followed each other rapidly through his head.

'Dislike? Hate? Yes, that's true enough. Should I be glad

116

if she died tomorrow? My God, yes! I'd feel like a man who's been let out of prison. What a queer beastly business life is! When I first saw her in *Do It Now*, what a child, what an adorable child she looked! So fair and so lovely . . . Damned young fool! I was mad about her – crazy . . . She seemed everything that was adorable and sweet, and all the time she was what she is now – vulgar, vicious, spiteful, empty-headed . . . I can't even see her loveliness now.'

He whistled and a spaniel came running to him, looking up at him with adoring sentimental eyes.

He said, 'Good old Betsy,' and fondled the long, fringed ears.

He thought, 'Funny term of disparagement, to call a woman a bitch. A bitch like you, Betsy, is worth nearly all the women I've met put together.'

Cramming an old fishing hat on his head, he left the house accompanied by the dog.

This aimless saunter of his round the estate began gradually to soothe his jangled nerves. He stroked the neck of his favourite hunter, had a word with the groom, then he went to the Home Farm and had a chat with the farmer's wife. He was walking along a narrow lane, Betsy at his heels, when he met Venetia Kerr on her bay mare.

Venetia looked her best upon a horse. Lord Horbury looked up at her with admiration, fondness and a queer sense of homecoming.

He said, 'Hullo, Venetia.'

'Hullo, Stephen.'

'Where've you been? Out in the five-acre?'

'Yes, she's coming along nicely, isn't she?'

'First-rate. Have you seen that two-year-old of mine I bought at Chattisley's sale?'

They talked horses for some minutes, then he said:

'By the way, Cicely's here.'

'Here, at Horbury?'

117

Against Venetia's code to show surprise, but she could not quite keep the undertone of it out of her voice.

'Yes. Turned up last night.'

There was a silence between them. Then Stephen said, 'You were at that inquest, Venetia. How – how – er – did it go?'

She considered a moment.

'Well, nobody was saying very much, if you know what I mean.'

'Police weren't giving anything away?'

'No.'

Stephen said, 'Must have been rather an unpleasant business for you.'

'Well, I didn't exactly enjoy it. But it wasn't too devastating. The coroner was quite decent.'

Stephen slashed absent-mindedly at the hedge.

'I say, Venetia, any idea – have *you*, I mean – as to who did it?'

Venetia Kerr shook her head slowly.

'No.' She paused a minute, seeking how best and most tactfully to put into words what she wanted to say. She achieved it at last with a little laugh. 'Anyway, it wasn't Cicely or me. That I do know. She'd have spotted me and I'd have spotted her.'

Stephen laughed too.

'That's all right, then,' he said cheerfully.

He passed it off as a joke, but she heard the relief in his voice. So he *had* been thinking –

She switched her thoughts away.

'Venetia,' said Stephen, 'I've known you a long time, haven't I?'

'H'm, yes. Do you remember those awful dancing classes we used to go to as children?'

'Do I not? I feel I can say things to you –'

'Of course you can.' She hesitated, then went on in a calm, matter-of-fact tone: 'It's Cicely, I suppose?'

'Yes. Look here, Venetia. Was Cicely mixed up with this woman Giselle in any way?'

Venetia answered slowly.

'I don't know. I've been in the South of France, remember. I haven't heard the Le Pinet gossip yet.'

'What do you think?'

'Well, candidly, I shouldn't be surprised.'

Stephen nodded thoughtfully. Venetia said gently:

'Need it worry you? I mean you live pretty semi-detached lives, don't you? This business is her affair, not yours.'

'As long as she's my wife, it's bound to be my business too.'

'Can't you – er – agree to a divorce?'

'A trumped-up business, you mean? I doubt if she'd accept it.'

'Would you divorce her if you had the chance?'

'If I had a cause I certainly would.'

He spoke grimly.

'I suppose,' said Venetia thoughtfully, 'she knows that.'

'Yes.'

They were both silent. Venetia thought, 'She has the morals of a cat! I know that well enough. But she's careful. She's shrewd as they make 'em.' Aloud she said, 'So there's nothing doing?'

He shook his head. Then he said, 'If I were free, Venetia, would you marry me?'

Looking very straight between her horse's ears, Venetia said in a voice carefully devoid of emotion:

'I suppose I would.'

Stephen! She'd always loved Stephen, always since the old days of dancing classes and cubbing and birds' nesting. And Stephen had been fond of her, but not fond enough to prevent him from falling desperately, wildly, madly in love with a clever calculating cat of a chorus girl . . .

Stephen said, 'We could have a marvellous life together . . .'

Pictures floated before his eyes: hunting – tea and muffins – the smell of wet earth and leaves – children . . . All the things that Cicely could never share with him, that Cicely would never give him. A kind of mist came over his eyes. Then he heard Venetia speaking, still in that flat, emotionless voice:

'Stephen, if you care – what about it? If we went off together Cicely would have to divorce you.'

He interrupted her fiercely. 'My God, do you think I'd let you do a thing like that?'

'I shouldn't care.'

'I should.'

He spoke with finality.

Venetia thought, 'That's that. It's a pity, really. He's hopelessly prejudiced, but rather a dear. I wouldn't like him to be different.'

Aloud she said, 'Well, Stephen, I'll be getting along.'

She touched her horse gently with her heel. As she turned to wave goodbye to Stephen their eyes met, and in that glance was all the feeling that their careful words had avoided.

As she rounded the corner of the lane Venetia dropped her whip. A man walking picked it up and returned it to her with an exaggerated bow.

'A foreigner,' she thought as she thanked him. 'I seem to remember his face.' Half of her mind searched through the summer days at Juan les Pins while the other half thought of Stephen.

Only just as she reached home did memory suddenly pull her half-dreaming brain up with a jerk.

'*The little man who gave me his seat in the aeroplane. They said at the inquest he was a detective.*' And hard on that came another thought: '*What is he doing down here?*'

CHAPTER 13

At Antoine's

Jane presented herself at Antoine's on the morning after the inquest with some trepidation of spirit.

The person who was usually regarded as M. Antoine himself, and whose real name was Andrew Leech and whose claims to foreign nationality consisted of having had a Jewish mother, greeted her with an ominous frown.

It was by now second nature to him to speak in broken English once within the portals of Bruton Street.

He upbraided Jane as a complete *imbécile*. Why did she wish to travel by air, anyway? What an idea! Her escapade would do his establishment infinite harm. Having vented his spleen to the full, Jane was permitted to escape, receiving as she did so a large-sized wink from her friend Gladys.

Gladys was an ethereal blonde with a haughty demeanour and a faint, far-away professional voice. In private her voice was hoarse and jocular.

'Don't you worry, dear,' she said to Jane. 'The old brute's sitting on the fence watching which way the cat will jump. And it's my belief it isn't going to jump the way he thinks it is. Ta ta, dearie, here's my old devil coming in, damn her eyes. I suppose she'll be in seventeen tantrums as usual. I hope she hasn't brought that damned lap-dog with her.'

A moment later Gladys's voice could be heard with its faint, far-away notes . . .

'Good morning, Madam, not brought your sweet little Pekingese with you? Shall we get on with the shampoo, and then we'll be all ready for M. Henri.'

Jane had just entered the adjoining cubicle where a

henna-haired woman was sitting waiting, examining her face in the glass and saying to a friend:

'Darling, my face is really *too* frightful this morning, it really is . . .'

The friend, who in a bored manner was turning over the pages of a three-weeks-old *Sketch*, replied uninterestedly:

'Do you think so, my sweet? It seems to me much the same as usual.'

On the entrance of Jane the bored friend stopped her languid survey of the *Sketch* and subjected Jane to a piercing stare instead.

Then she said, 'It is, darling. I'm sure of it.'

'Good morning, Madam,' said Jane with that airy brightness expected of her and which she could now produce quite mechanically and without any effort whatsoever. 'It's quite a long time since we've seen you here. I expect you've been abroad.'

'Antibes,' said the henna-haired woman, who in her turn was staring at Jane with the frankest interest.

'How lovely,' said Jane with false enthusiasm. 'Let me see, is it a shampoo and set, or are you having a tint today?'

Momentarily diverted from her scrutiny, the henna-haired woman leaned forward and examined her hair attentively.

'I think I could go another week. Heavens, what a fright I look!'

The friend said, 'Well, darling, what can you expect at this time of the morning?'

Jane said, 'Ah! wait until M. Georges has finished with you.'

'Tell me,' the woman resumed her stare, 'are you the girl who gave evidence at the inquest yesterday – the girl who was in the aeroplane?'

'Yes, Madam.'

'How too terribly thrilling! Tell me about it.'

Jane did her best to please.

122

'Well, Madam, it was all rather dreadful, really –' She plunged into narration, answering questions as they came. What had the old woman looked like? Was it true that there were two French detectives aboard and that the whole thing was mixed up with the French Government scandals? Was Lady Horbury on board? Was she really as good-looking as everyone said? Who did she, Jane, think had actually done the murder? They said the whole thing was being hushed up for Government reasons, and so on and so on . . .

This first ordeal was only a forerunner of many others all on the same lines. Everyone wanted to be done by 'the girl who was on the plane.' Everyone was able to say to their friends, 'My dear, positively too marvellous. The girl at my hairdresser's is *the* girl . . . Yes, I should go there if I were you – they do your hair very well . . . Jeanne, her name is . . . rather a little thing, big eyes. She'll tell you all about it if you ask her nicely . . .'

By the end of the week Jane felt her nerves giving way under the strain. Sometimes she felt that if she had to go through the recital once again she would scream or attack her questioner with the dryer.

However, in the end she hit upon a better way of relieving her feelings. She approached M. Antoine and boldly demanded a rise of salary.

'You ask that? You have the impudence, when it is only out of kindness of heart that I keep you here, after you have been mixed up in a murder case? Many men, less kindhearted than I, would have dismissed you immediately.'

'That's nonsense,' said Jane coolly. 'I'm a draw in this place and you know it. If you want me to go, I'll go. I'll easily get what I want from Henri's or the Maison Richet.'

'And who is to know you have gone there? Of what importance are you anyway?'

'I met one or two reporters at that inquest,' said Jane. 'One of them would give my change of establishment any publicity needed.'

Because he feared that this was indeed so, grumblingly M. Antoine agreed to Jane's demands. Gladys applauded her friend heartily.

'Good for you, dear,' she said. 'Ikey Andrew was no match for you that time. If a girl couldn't fend for herself a bit I don't know where we'd all be. Grit, dear, that's what you've got, and I admire you for it.'

'I can fight for my own hand all right,' said Jane, her small chin lifting itself pugnaciously. 'I've had to all my life.'

'Hard lines, dear,' said Gladys. 'But keep your end up with Ikey Andrew. He likes you all the better for it, really. Meekness doesn't pay in this life – but I don't think we're either of us troubled by too much of that.'

Thereafter Jane's narrative, repeated daily with little variation, sank into the equivalent of a part played on the stage.

The promised dinner and theatre with Norman Gale had duly come off. It was one of those enchanting evenings when every word and confidence exchanged seemed to reveal a bond of sympathy and shared tastes.

They liked dogs and disliked cats. They both hated oysters and loved smoked salmon. They liked Greta Garbo and disliked Katharine Hepburn. They didn't like fat women and admired really jet-black hair. They disliked very red nails. They disliked loud voices, noisy restaurants and negroes. They preferred buses to tubes.

It seemed almost miraculous that two people should have so many points of agreement.

One day at Antoine's, opening her bag, Jane let a letter from Norman fall out. As she picked it up with a slightly heightened colour, Gladys pounced upon her.

'Who's your boy friend, dear?'

'I don't know what you mean,' retorted Jane, her colour rising.

'Don't tell me! I know that letter isn't from your mother's great-uncle. I wasn't born yesterday. Who is he, Jane?'

'It's someone – a man – that I met at Le Pinet. He's a dentist.'

'A dentist,' said Gladys with lively distaste. 'I suppose he's got very white teeth and a smile.'

Jane was forced to admit that this was indeed the case.

'He's got a very brown face and very blue eyes.'

'Anyone can have a brown face,' said Gladys. 'It may be the seaside or it may come out of a bottle, 2s. 11d. at the chemist's. *Handsome Men are Slightly Bronzed*. The eyes sound all right. But a dentist! Why, if he was going to kiss you you'd feel he was going to say, "Open a little wider, please".'

'Don't be an idiot, Gladys.'

'You needn't be so touchy, my dear. I see you've got it badly. Yes, Mr Henry, I'm just coming . . . Drat Henry! Thinks he's God Almighty, the way he orders us girls about!'

The letter had been to suggest dinner on Saturday evening. At lunch-time on Saturday when Jane received her augmented pay she felt full of high spirits.

'And to think,' said Jane to herself, 'that I was worrying so that day coming over in the aeroplane. Everything's turned out beautifully . . . Life is really too marvellous.'

So full of exuberance did she feel that she decided to be extravagant and lunch at the Corner House and enjoy the accompaniment of music to her food.

She seated herself at a table for four, where there were already a middle-aged woman and a young man sitting. The middle-aged woman was just finishing her lunch. Presently she called for her bill, picked up a large collection of parcels and departed.

Jane, as was her custom, read a book as she ate. Looking up as she turned a page, she noticed the young man opposite her staring at her very intently, and at the same moment realized that his face was vaguely familiar to her.

Just as she made these discoveries the young man caught her eye and bowed.

'Excuse me, Mademoiselle, you not recognize me?'

Jane looked at him more attentively. He had a fair boyish-looking face, attractive more by reason of its extreme mobility than because of any actual claim to good looks.

'We have not been introduced, it is true,' went on the young man, 'unless you call murder an introduction and the fact that we both gave evidence in the coroner's court.'

'Of course,' said Jane. 'How stupid of me! I thought I knew your face. You are –?'

'Jean Dupont,' said the man and gave a funny, rather engaging little bow.

A remembrance flashed into Jane's mind of a dictum of Gladys's, expressed perhaps without undue delicacy.

'If there's one fellow after you, there's sure to be another. Seems to be a law of Nature. Sometimes it's three or four.'

Now Jane had always led an austere, hard-working life (rather like the description after the act of girls who were missing – 'She was a bright, cheerful girl with no men friends, etc.'). Jane had been 'a bright, cheerful girl with no men friends'. Now it seemed that men friends were rolling up all round. There was no doubt about it, Jean Dupont's face as he leaned across the table held more than mere interested politeness. He was pleased to be sitting opposite Jane. He was more than pleased – he was delighted.

Jane thought to herself with a touch of misgiving:

'He's French, though. You've got to look out with the French, they always say so.'

'You're still in England, then,' said Jane, and silently cursed herself for the extreme inanity of her remark.

'Yes. My father has been to Edinburgh to give a lecture there, and we have stayed with friends also. But now – tomorrow – we return to France.'

'I see.'

126

'The police, they have not made an arrest yet?' said Jean Dupont.

'No, there's not even been anything about it in the papers lately. Perhaps they've given it up.'

Jean Dupont shook his head. 'No, no, they will not have given it up. They work silently' – he made an expressive gesture – 'in the dark.'

'Don't,' said Jane uneasily. 'You give me the creeps.'

'Yes, it is not a very nice feeling, to have been so close when a murder was committed . . .' He added, 'And I was closer than you were. I was very close indeed. Sometimes I do not like to think of that . . .'

'Who do you think did it?' asked Jane. 'I've wondered and wondered.'

Jean Dupont shrugged his shoulders.

'It was not I. She was far too ugly!'

'Well,' said Jane, 'I suppose you would rather kill an ugly woman than a good-looking one?'

'Not at all. If a woman is good-looking you are fond of her – she treats you badly – she makes you jealous, mad with jealousy. "Good," you say, "I will kill her. It will be a satisfaction".'

'And is it a satisfaction?'

'That, Mademoiselle, I do not know, because I have not yet tried.' He laughed, then shook his head. 'But an ugly old woman like Giselle – who would want to bother to kill her?'

'Well, that's one way of looking at it,' said Jane. She frowned. 'It seems rather terrible, somehow, to think that perhaps she was young and pretty once.'

'I know, I know.' He became suddenly grave. 'It is the great tragedy of life, that women grow old.'

'You seem to think a lot about women and their looks,' said Jane.

'Naturally. It is the most interesting subject possible. That seems strange to you because you are English. An Englishman thinks first of his work – his job, he calls it –

127

and then of his sport, and last – a good way last – of his
wife. Yes, yes, it is really so. Why, imagine, in a little
hotel in Syria was an Englishman whose wife had been
taken ill. He himself had to be somewhere in Iraq by a
certain date. *Eh bien*, would you believe it, he left his wife
and went on so as to be "on duty" in time. And both he
and his wife thought that quite natural; they thought him
noble, unselfish. But the doctor, who was not English,
thought him a barbarian. A wife, a human being – that
should come first; to do one's job – that is something much
less important.'

'I don't know,' said Jane. 'One's work has to come first,
I suppose.'

'But why? You see, you too have the same point of view.
By doing one's work one obtains money – by indulging
and looking after a woman one spends it – so the last is
much more noble an ideal than the first.'

Jane laughed.

'Oh, well,' she said. 'I think I'd rather be regarded as a
mere luxury and self-indulgence, than regarded sternly as a
First Duty. I'd rather a man felt that he was enjoying
himself looking after me than that he should feel I was a
duty to be attended to.'

'No one, Mademoiselle, would be likely to feel that with
you.'

Jane blushed slightly at the earnestness of the young
man's tone. He went on talking quickly:

'I have only been in England once before. It was very
interesting to me the other day at the – inquest, you call it?
– to study three young and charming women, all so
different from one another.'

'What did you think of us all?' asked Jane, amused.

'That Lady Horbury – bah, I know her type well. It is
very exotic – very, very expensive. You see it sitting round
the baccarat table – the soft face – the hard expression –
and you know – you know so well what it will be like in,

128

say fifteen years. She lives for sensation, that one. For high play, perhaps for drugs . . . *Au fond*, she is uninteresting!'

'And Miss Kerr?'

'Ah, she is very, very English. She is the kind that any shopkeeper on the Riviera will give credit to; they are very discerning, our shopkeepers. Her clothes are very well cut, but rather like a man's. She walks about as though she owns the earth. She is not conceited about it – she is just an Englishwoman. She knows which department of England different people come from. It is true. I have heard ones like her in Egypt. "What? The Etceteras are here? The Yorkshire Etceteras? Oh, the Shropshire Etceteras".'

His mimicry was good. Jane laughed at the drawling, well-bred tones.

'And then – me,' she said.

'And then you. And I say to myself, "How nice, how very nice it would be if I were to see her again one day." And here I am sitting opposite you. The gods arrange things very well sometimes.'

Jane said, 'You're an archaeologist, aren't you? You dig up things?'

And she listened with keen attention while Jean Dupont talked of his work.

Jane gave a little sigh at last.

'You've been in so many countries. You've seen so much. It all sounds so fascinating. And I shall never go anywhere or see anything.'

'You would like that – to go abroad – to see wild parts of the earth? You would not be able to get your hair waved, remember.'

'It waves by itself,' said Jane, laughing.

She looked up at the clock and hastily summoned the waitress for her bill.

Jean Dupont said with a little embarrassment, 'Mademoiselle, I wonder if you would permit – as I have told you, I return to France tomorrow – if you would dine with me tonight.'

'I'm so sorry, I can't. I'm dining with someone.'

'Ah! I'm sorry, very sorry. You will come again to Paris, soon?'

'I don't expect so.'

'And me, I do not know when I shall be in London again! It is sad?'

He stood a moment, holding Jane's hand in his.

'I shall hope to see you again, very much,' he said, and sounded as though he meant it.

CHAPTER 14

At Muswell Hill

At about the time that Jane was leaving Antoine's, Norman Gale was saying in a hearty professional tone, 'Just a little tender, I'm afraid . . . Guide me if I hurt you –'

His expert hand guided the electric drill.

'There, that's all over. Miss Ross?'

Miss Ross was immediately at his elbow stirring a minute white concoction on a slab.

Norman Gale completed his filling and said, 'Let me see, it's next Tuesday you're coming for those others?'

His patient, rinsing her mouth ardently, burst into a fluent explanation. She was going away – so sorry – would have to cancel the next appointment. Yes, she would let him know when she got back.

And she escaped hurriedly from the room.

'Well,' said Gale, 'that's all for today.'

Miss Ross said, 'Lady Higginson rang up to say she must give up her appointment next week. She wouldn't make another. Oh, and Colonel Blunt can't come on Thursday.'

Norman Gale nodded. His face hardened.

Every day was the same. People ringing up. Cancelled appointments. All varieties of excuses – going away – going abroad – got a cold – may not be here –

It didn't matter what reason they gave, the real reason Norman had just seen quite unmistakably in his last patient's eye as he reached for the drill . . . a look of sudden panic . . .

He could have written down the woman's thoughts on paper.

'Oh, dear, of course he was in that aeroplane when that woman was murdered . . . I wonder . . . You do hear of people going off their heads and doing the most senseless crimes. It really isn't safe. The man might be a homicidal lunatic. They look the same as other people, I've always heard . . . I believe I always felt there was rather a peculiar look in his eye . . .'

'Well,' said Gale, 'it looks like being a quiet week next week, Miss Ross.'

'Yes, a lot of people have dropped out. Oh, well, you can do with a rest. You worked so hard earlier in the summer.'

'It doesn't look as though I were going to have a chance of working very hard in the autumn, does it?'

Miss Ross did not reply. She was saved from having to do so by the telephone ringing. She went out of the room to answer it.

Norman dropped some instruments into the sterilizer, thinking hard.

'Let's see how we stand. No beating about the bush. This business has about done for me professionally. Funny, it's done well for Jane. People come on purpose to gape at her. Come to think of it, that's what's wrong here – they *have* to gape at me, and they don't like it! Nasty helpless feeling you have in a dentist's chair. If the dentist were to run amuck . . .

'What a strange business murder is! You'd think it was a perfectly straightforward issue – and it isn't. It affects all sorts of queer things you'd never think of . . . Come back to facts. As a dentist I seem to be about done for . . . What would happen, I wonder, if they arrested the Horbury woman? Would my patients come trooping back? Hard to say. Once the rot's set in . . . Oh, well, what does it matter? I don't care. Yes, I do – because of Jane . . . Jane's adorable. I want her. And I can't have her – yet . . . A damnable nuisance.'

He smiled. 'I feel it's going to be all right . . . She cares . . . She'll wait . . . Damn it, I shall go to Canada – yes, that's it – and make money there.'

He laughed to himself.

Miss Ross came back into the room.

'That was Mrs Lorrie. She's sorry –'

'– but she may be going to Timbuctoo,' finished Norman. '*Vive les rats!* You'd better look out for another post, Miss Ross. This seems to be a sinking ship.'

'Oh, Mr Gale, I shouldn't think of deserting you . . .'

'Good girl. You're not a rat, anyway. But seriously I mean it. If something doesn't happen to clear up this mess I'm done for.'

'Something *ought* to be done about it!' said Miss Ross with energy. 'I think the police are *disgraceful*. They're not *trying*.'

Norman laughed. 'I expect they're trying all right.'

'Somebody ought to do something.'

'Quite right. I've rather thought of trying to do something myself – though I don't quite know what.'

'Oh, Mr Gale, I should. You're so clever.'

'I'm a hero to that girl all right,' thought Norman Gale. 'She'd like to help me in my sleuth stuff; but I've got another partner in view.'

It was that same evening that he dined with Jane. Half-unconsciously he pretended to be in very high spirits, but Jane was too astute to be deceived. She noted his sudden moments of absent-mindedness, the little frown that showed between his brows, the sudden strained line of his mouth.

She said at last, 'Norman, are things going badly?'

He shot a quick glance at her, then looked away.

'Well, not too frightfully well. It's a bad time of year.'

'Don't be idiotic,' said Jane sharply.

'Jane!'

'I mean it. Don't you think I can see that you're worried to death?'

'I'm not worried to death. I'm just annoyed.'

'You mean people are fighting shy –'

'Of having their teeth attended to by a possible murderer? Yes.'

'How cruelly unfair!'

'It is, rather. Because frankly, Jane, I'm a jolly good dentist. And I'm not a murderer.'

'It's wicked. Somebody ought to do something.'

'That's what my secretary, Miss Ross, said this morning.'

'What's she like?'

'Miss Ross?'

'Yes.'

'Oh, I don't know. Big – lots of bones – nose rather like a rocking horse – frightfully competent.'

'She sounds quite nice,' said Jane graciously.

Norman rightly took this as a tribute to his diplomacy. Miss Ross's bones were not really quite as formidable as stated, and she had an extremely attractive head of red hair, but he felt, and rightly, that it was just as well not to dwell on the latter point to Jane.

'I'd like to do *something*,' he said. 'If I was a young man in a book I'd find a clue or I'd shadow somebody.'

Jane tugged suddenly at his sleeve.

'Look, there's Mr Clancy – you know, the author – sitting over there by the wall by himself. We might shadow him.'

'But we were going to the flicks?'

'Never mind the flicks. I feel somehow this might be *meant*. You said you wanted to shadow somebody, and here's somebody to shadow. You never know. We might find out something.'

Jane's enthusiasm was infectious. Norman fell in with the plan readily enough.

'As you say, one never knows,' he said. 'Whereabouts has he got to in his dinner? I can't see properly without turning my head, and I don't want to stare.'

'He's about level with us,' said Jane. 'We'd better hurry a bit and get ahead and then we can pay the bill and be ready to leave when he does.'

They adopted this plan. When at last little Mr Clancy rose and passed out into Dean Street, Norman and Jane were fairly close on his heels.

'In case he takes a taxi,' Jane explained.

But Mr Clancy did not take a taxi. Carrying an overcoat over one arm (and occasionally allowing it to trail on the ground), he ambled gently through the London streets. His progress was somewhat erratic. Sometimes he moved forward at a brisk trot, sometimes he slowed down till he almost came to a stop. Once, on the very brink of crossing a road, he did come to a standstill, standing there with one foot hanging over the kerb and looking exactly like a slow-motion picture.

His direction, too, was erratic. Once he actually took so many right-angle turns that he traversed the same streets twice over.

Jane felt her spirits rise.

'You see?' she said excitedly. 'He's afraid of being followed. He's trying to put us off the scent.'

'Do you think so?'

'Of course. Nobody would go round in circles otherwise.'

'Oh!'

They had turned a corner rather quickly and had almost cannoned into their quarry. He was standing staring up at a butcher's shop. The shop itself was naturally closed, but it seemed to be something about the level of the first floor that was riveting Mr Clancy's attention.

He said aloud, 'Perfect. The very thing. What a piece of luck!'

He took out a little book and wrote something down very carefully. Then he started off again at a brisk pace, humming a little tune.

He was now heading definitely for Bloomsbury. Sometimes, when he turned his head, the two behind could see his lips moving.

'There is something up,' said Jane. 'He's in great distress of mind. He's talking to himself and he doesn't know it.'

As he waited to cross by some traffic lights, Norman and Jane drew abreast.

It was quite true; Mr Clancy was talking to himself. His face looked white and strained. Norman and Jane caught a few muttered words:

'Why doesn't she speak? Why? There must be a *reason* . . .'

The lights went green. As they reached the opposite pavement Mr Clancy said, 'I see now. Of course. That's why she's got to be silenced!'

Jane pinched Norman ferociously.

Mr Clancy set off at a great pace now. The overcoat dragged hopelessly. With great strides the little author covered the ground, apparently oblivious of the two people on his tracks.

Finally, with disconcerting abruptness, he stopped at a house, opened the door with a key and went in.

Norman and Jane looked at each other.

'It's his own house,' said Norman. '47 Cardington Square. That's the address he gave at the inquest.'

'Oh, well,' said Jane, 'perhaps he'll come out again by and by. And, anyway, we have heard *something*. Somebody – a woman – is going to be silenced, and some other woman won't speak. Oh, dear, it sounds dreadfully like a detective story.'

A voice came out of the darkness. 'Good evening,' it said.

The owner of the voice stepped forward. A pair of magnificent moustaches showed in the lamplight.

'*Eh bien*,' said Hercule Poirot. 'A fine evening for the chase, is it not?'

CHAPTER 15

In Bloomsbury

Of the two startled young people, it was Norman Gale who recovered himself first.

'Of course,' he said, 'it's Monsieur – Monsieur Poirot. Are you still trying to clear your character, M. Poirot?'

'Ah, you remember our little conversation? And it is the poor Mr Clancy you suspect?'

'So do you,' said Jane acutely, 'or you wouldn't be here.'

He looked at her thoughtfully for a moment.

'Have you ever thought about murder, Mademoiselle? Thought about it, I mean, in the abstract – cold-bloodedly and dispassionately?'

'I don't think I've ever thought about it at all until just lately,' said Jane.

Hercule Poirot nodded.

'Yes, you think about it now because a murder has touched you personally. But me, I have dealt with crime for many years now. I have my own way of regarding things. What should you say the most important thing was to bear in mind when you are trying to solve a murder?'

'Finding the murderer,' said Jane.

Norman Gale said, 'Justice.'

Poirot shook his head. 'There are more important things than finding the murderer. And justice is a fine word, but it is sometimes difficult to say exactly what one means by it. In my opinion the important thing is to clear the innocent.'

'Oh, naturally,' said Jane. 'That goes without saying. If anyone is falsely accused –'

'Not even that. *There may be no accusation.* But until one person is proved guilty beyond any possible doubt, everyone else who is associated with the crime is liable to suffer in varying degrees.'

Norman Gale said with emphasis, 'How true that is.'

Jane said, 'Don't we know it!'

Poirot looked from one to the other.

'I see. Already you have been finding that out for yourselves.'

He became suddenly brisk.

'Come now, I have affairs to see to. Since our aims are the same, we three, let us combine together. I am about to call upon our ingenious friend, Mr Clancy. I would suggest that Mademoiselle accompanies me – in the guise of my secretary. Here, Mademoiselle, is a notebook and a pencil for the shorthand.'

'I can't write shorthand,' gasped Jane.

'But naturally not. But you have the quick wits – the intelligence – you can make plausible signs in pencil in the book, can you not? Good. As for Mr Gale, I suggest that he meets us in, say, an hour's time. Shall we say upstairs at Monseigneur's? *Bon!* We will compare notes then.'

And forthwith he advanced to the bell and pressed it.

Slightly dazed, Jane followed him, clutching the notebook.

Gale opened his mouth as though to protest, then seemed to think better of it.

'Right,' he said. 'In an hour, at Monseigneur's.'

The door was opened by a rather forbidding-looking elderly woman attired in severe black.

Poirot said, 'Mr Clancy?'

She drew back and Poirot and Jane entered.

'What name sir?'

'Mr Hercule Poirot.'

The severe woman led them upstairs and into a room on the first floor.

'Mr Air Kule Prott,' she announced.

Poirot realized at once the force of Mr Clancy's announcement at Croydon to the effect that he was not a tidy man. The room, a long one, with three windows along its length and shelves and bookcases on the other walls, was in a state of chaos. There were papers strewn about, cardboard files, bananas, bottles of beer, open books, sofa cushions, a trombone, miscellaneous china, etchings, and a bewildering assortment of fountain-pens.

In the middle of this confusion Mr Clancy was struggling with a camera and a roll of films.

'Dear me,' said Mr Clancy, looking up as the visitors were announced. He put the camera down and the roll of films promptly fell on the floor and unwound itself. He came forward with outstretched hand. 'Very glad to see you, I'm sure.'

'You remember me, I hope?' said Poirot. 'This is my secretary, Miss Grey.'

'How d'you do, Miss Grey.' He shook her by the hand and then turned back to Poirot. 'Yes, of course I remember you – at least – now, where was it exactly? Was it at the Skull and Crossbones Club?'

'We were fellow-passengers on an aeroplane from Paris on a certain fatal occasion.'

'Why, of course,' said Mr Clancy. 'And Miss Grey too! Only I hadn't realized she was your secretary. In fact, I had some idea that she was in a beauty parlour – something of that kind.'

Jane looked anxiously at Poirot.

The latter was quite equal to the situation.

'Perfectly correct,' he said. 'As an efficient secretary, Miss Grey has at times to undertake certain work of a temporary nature – you understand?'

'Of course,' said Mr Clancy. 'I was forgetting. You're a detective – the real thing. Not Scotland Yard. Private investigation. Do sit down, Miss Grey. No, not there; I think there's orange juice on that chair. If I shift this file – Oh, dear, now everything's tumbled out. Never mind. You sit

139

here, M. Poirot – that's right, isn't it? – Poirot? The back's not *really* broken. It only creaks a little as you lean against it. Well, perhaps it's best not to lean *too* hard. Yes, a private investigator like my Wilbraham Rice. The public have taken very strongly to Wilbraham Rice. He bites his nails and eats a lot of bananas. I don't know why I made him bite his nails to start with – it's really rather disgusting – but there it is. He started by biting his nails, and now he has to do it in every single book. So monotonous. The bananas aren't so bad; you get a bit of fun out of them – criminals slipping on the skin. I eat bananas myself – that's what put it into my head. But I don't bite my nails. Have some beer?'

'I thank you, no.'

Mr Clancy sighed, sat down himself, and gazed earnestly at Poirot.

'I can guess what you've come about – the murder of Giselle. I've thought and thought about that case. You can say what you like, it's amazing – poisoned darts and a blowpipe in an aeroplane. An idea I have used myself, as I told you, both in book and short story form. Of course it was a very shocking occurrence, but I must confess, M. Poirot, that I was thrilled, positively thrilled.'

'I can quite see,' said Poirot, 'that the crime must have appealed to you professionally, Mr Clancy.'

Mr Clancy beamed.

'Exactly. You would think that anyone – even the official police – could have understood that! But not at all. Suspicion – that is all I got, both from the inspector and at the inquest. I go out of my way to assist the course of justice, and all I get for my pains is palpable thick-headed suspicion!'

'All the same,' said Poirot, smiling, 'it does not seem to affect you very much.'

'Ah,' said Mr Clancy. 'But, you see, I have my methods, Watson. If you'll excuse my calling you Watson. No offence intended. Interesting, by the way, how the technique of the idiot friend has hung on. Personally I myself think the Sherlock Holmes stories grossly overrated. The fallacies – the really amazing fallacies that there are in those stories – But what was I saying?'

'You said that you had your methods.'

'Ah, yes.' Mr Clancy leaned forward. 'I'm putting that inspector – what is his name, Japp? – yes, I'm putting him in my next book. You should see the way Wilbraham Rice deals with him.'

'In between bananas, as one might say.'

'In between bananas – that's very good, that.' Mr Clancy chuckled.

'You have a great advantage as a writer, Monsieur,' said Poirot. 'You can relieve your feelings by the expedient of the printed word. You have the power of the pen over your enemies.'

Mr Clancy rocked gently back in his chair.

'You know,' he said, 'I begin to think this murder is going to be a really fortunate thing for me. I'm writing the whole thing exactly as it happened – only as fiction, of course, and I shall call it *The Air Mail Mystery*. Perfect pen portraits of all the passengers. It ought to sell like wildfire – if only I can get it out in time.'

'Won't you be had up for libel, or something?' asked Jane.

Mr Clancy turned a beaming face upon her.

'No, no, my dear lady. Of course, if I were to make one of the passengers the murderer – well, then, I might be liable for damages. But that is the strong part of it all – an entirely unexpected solution is revealed in the last chapter.'

Poirot leaned forward eagerly.

'And that solution is?'

Again Mr Clancy chuckled.

'Ingenious,' he said. 'Ingenious and sensational. Disguised as the pilot, a girl gets into the plane at Le Bourget and successfully stows herself away under Madame Giselle's seat. She has with her an ampoule of the newest gas. She releases this – everybody becomes unconscious for three minutes – she squirms out – fires the poisoned dart, and makes a parachute descent from the rear door of the car.'

Both Jane and Poirot blinked.

Jane said, 'Why doesn't she become unconscious from the gas too?'

'Respirator,' said Mr Clancy.

'And she descends into the Channel?'

'It needn't be the Channel – I shall make it the French coast.'

'And, anyway, nobody could hide under a seat; there wouldn't be room.'

'There will be room in my aeroplane,' said Mr Clancy firmly.

'*Epatant*,' said Poirot. 'And the motive of the lady?'

'I haven't quite decided,' said Mr Clancy meditatively. 'Probably Giselle ruined the girl's lover, who killed himself.'

'And how did she get hold of the poison?'

'That's the really clever part,' said Mr Clancy. 'The girl's a snake charmer. She extracts the stuff from her favourite python.'

'*Mon Dieu!*' said Hercule Poirot.

He said, 'You don't think, perhaps, it is just a *little* sensational.'

'You can't write anything too sensational,' said Mr Clancy firmly. 'Especially when you're dealing with the arrow poison of the South American Indians. I know it was snake juice, really; but the principle is the same. After all, you don't want a detective story to be like real life? Look at the things in the papers – dull as ditchwater.'

'Come, now, Monsieur, would you say this little affair of ours is dull as ditchwater?'

'No,' admitted Mr Clancy. 'Sometimes, you know, I can't believe it really happened.'

Poirot drew the creaking chair a little nearer to his host. His voice lowered itself confidentially.

'M. Clancy, you are a man of brains and imagination. The police, as you say, have regarded you with suspicion. They have not sought your advice. But I, Hercule Poirot, desire to consult you.'

Mr Clancy flushed with pleasure.

'I'm sure that's very nice of you.'

He looked flustered and pleased.

'You have studied the criminology. Your ideas will be of value. It would be of great interest to me to know who, in your opinion, committed the crime.'

'Well –' Mr Clancy hesitated, reached automatically for a banana and began to eat it. Then, the animation dying out of his face, he shook his head. 'You see, M. Poirot, it's an entirely different thing. When you're writing you can make it anyone you like; but, of course, in real life there is a real person. You haven't any command over the facts. I'm afraid, you know, that I'd be absolutely no good as a real detective.'

He shook his head sadly and threw the banana skin into the grate.

'It might be amusing, however, to consider the case together?' suggested Poirot.

'Oh, that, yes.'

'To begin with, supposing you had to make a sporting guess, who would you choose?'

'Oh, well, I suppose one of the two Frenchmen.'

'Now, why?'

'Well, she was French. It seems more likely, somehow. And they were sitting on the opposite side not too far away from her. But really I don't know.'

'It depends,' said Poirot thoughtfully, 'so much on motive.'

'Of course – of course. I suppose you tabulate all the motives very scientifically?'

'I am old-fashioned in my methods. I follow the old adage: seek whom the crime benefits.'

'That's all very well,' said Mr Clancy. 'But I take it that's a little difficult in a case like this. There's a daughter who comes into money, so I've heard. But a lot of the people on board might benefit, for all we know – that is if they owed her money and haven't got to pay it back.'

'True,' said Poirot. 'And I can think of other solutions. Let us suppose that Madame Giselle knew of something – attempted murder, shall we say? – on the part of one of those people.'

'Attempted murder?' said Mr Clancy. 'Now, why attempted murder? What a very curious suggestion.'

'In cases such as these,' said Poirot, 'one must think of everything.'

'Ah!' said Mr Clancy. 'But it's no good thinking. You've got to *know*.'

'You have reason – you have reason. A very just observation.'

Then he said, 'I ask your pardon, but this blowpipe that you bought –'

'Damn that blowpipe,' said Mr Clancy. 'I wish I'd never mentioned it.'

'You bought it, you say, at a shop in the Charing Cross Road? Do you, by any chance, remember the name of that shop?'

'Well,' said Mr Clancy, 'it might have been Absolom's – or there's Mitchell & Smith. I don't know. But I've already told all this to that pestilential inspector. He must have checked up on it by this time.'

'Ah,' said Poirot, 'but I ask for quite another reason. I desire to purchase such a thing and make a little experiment.'

'Oh, I see. But I don't know that you'll find one all the same. They don't keep sets of them, you know.'

'All the same I can try. Perhaps, Miss Grey, you would be so obliging as to take down those two names?'

Jane opened her notebook and rapidly performed a series of (she hoped) professional-looking squiggles. Then she surreptitiously wrote the names in longhand on the reverse side of the sheet in case these instructions of Poirot's should be genuine.

'And now,' said Poirot, 'I have trespassed on your time too long. I will take my departure with a thousand thanks for your amiability.'

'Not at all. Not at all,' said Mr Clancy. 'I wish you would have had a banana.'

'You are most amiable.'

'Not at all. As a matter of fact, I'm feeling rather happy tonight. I'd been held up in a short story I was writing – the thing wouldn't pan out properly, and I couldn't get a good name for the criminal. I wanted something with a flavour. Well, just a bit of luck, I saw just the name I wanted over a butcher's shop. Pargiter. Just the name I was looking for. There's a sort of genuine sound to it; and about five minutes later I got the other thing. There's always the same snag in stories – why won't the girl speak? The young man tries to make her and she says her lips are sealed. There's never any real reason, of course, why she shouldn't blurt out the whole thing at once, but you have to try to think of something that's not too definitely idiotic. Unfortunately it has to be a different thing every time!'

He smiled gently at Jane.

'The trials of an author!'

He darted past her to a bookcase.

'One thing you must allow me to give you.'

He came back with a book in his hand.

'*The Clue of the Scarlet Petal*. I think I mentioned at Croydon that that book of mine dealt with arrow poison and native darts.'

'A thousand thanks. You are too amiable.'

'Not at all. I see,' said Mr Clancy suddenly to Jane, 'that you don't use the Pitman system of shorthand.'

Jane flushed scarlet. Poirot came to her rescue.

'Miss Grey is very up to date. She uses the most recent system invented by a Czecho-Slovakian.'

'You don't say so? What an amazing place Czecho-Slovakia must be. Everything seems to come from there – shoes, glass, gloves, and now a shorthand system. Quite amazing.'

He shook hands with them both.

'I wish I could have been more helpful.'

They left him in the littered room smiling wistfully after them.

CHAPTER 16

Plan of Campaign

From Mr Clancy's house they took a taxi to the Monseigneur, where they found Norman Gale awaiting them.

Poirot ordered some *consommé* and a *chaud-froid* of chicken.

'Well?' said Norman. 'How did you get on?'

'Miss Grey,' said Poirot, 'has proved herself the super-secretary.'

'I don't think I did so very well,' said Jane. 'He spotted my stuff when he passed behind me. You know, he must be very observant.'

'Ah, you noticed that? This good Mr Clancy is not quite so absent-minded as one might imagine.'

'Did you really want those addresses?' asked Jane.

'I think they might be useful – yes.'

'But if the police –'

'Ah, the police! I should not ask the same questions as the police have asked. Though, as a matter of fact, I doubt whether the police have asked any questions at all. You see, they know that the blowpipe found in the plane was purchased in Paris by an American.'

'In Paris? An American? But there wasn't any American in the aeroplane.'

Poirot smiled kindly on her.

'Precisely. We have here an American just to make it more difficult. *Voilà tout.*'

'But it was bought by a man?' said Norman.

Poirot looked at him with rather an odd expression.

'Yes,' he said, 'it was *bought* by a man.'

Norman looked puzzled.

'Anyway,' said Jane, 'it wasn't Mr Clancy. He'd got one blowpipe already, so he wouldn't want to go about buying another.'

Poirot nodded his head.

'That is how one must proceed. Suspect everyone in turn and then wipe him or her off the list.'

'How many have you wiped off so far?' asked Jane.

'Not so many as you might think, Mademoiselle,' said Poirot with a twinkle. 'It depends, you see, on the motive.'

'Has there been –?' Norman Gale stopped and then added apologetically: 'I don't want to butt in on official secrets, but is there no record of this woman's dealings?'

Poirot shook his head.

'All the records are burnt.'

'That's unfortunate.'

'*Evidemment!* But it seems that Madame Giselle combined a little blackmailing with her profession of moneylending, and that opens up a wider field. Supposing, for instance, that Madame Giselle had knowledge of a certain criminal offence – say, attempted murder on the part of someone.'

'Is there any reason to suppose such a thing?'

'Why, yes,' said Poirot slowly. 'There is – one of the few pieces of documentary evidence that we have in this case.'

He looked from one to the other of their interested faces and gave a little sigh.

'Ah, well,' he said, 'that is that. Let us talk of other matters – for instance, of how this tragedy has affected the lives of you two young people.'

'It sounds horrible to say so, but I've done well out of it,' said Jane.

She related her rise of salary.

'As you say, Mademoiselle, you have done well, but probably only for the time being. Even a nine-days' wonder does not last longer than nine days, remember.'

Jane laughed. 'That's very true.'

148

'I'm afraid it's going to last more than nine days in my case,' said Norman.

He explained the position. Poirot listened sympathetically.

'As you say,' he observed thoughtfully, 'it will take more than nine days – or nine weeks – or nine months. Sensationalism dies quickly – fear is long-lived.'

'Do you think I ought to stick it out?'

'Have you any other plan?'

'Yes – chuck up the whole thing. Go out to Canada or somewhere and start again.'

'I'm sure that would be a pity,' said Jane firmly.

Norman looked at her.

Poirot tactfully became engrossed with his chicken.

'I don't want to go,' said Norman.

'If I discover who killed Madame Giselle, you will not have to go,' said Poirot cheerfully.

'Do you really think you will?' asked Jane.

Poirot looked at her reproachfully.

'If one approaches a problem with order and method there should be no difficulty in solving it – none whatever,' said Poirot severely.

'Oh, I see,' said Jane, who didn't.

'But I should solve this problem quicker if I had help,' said Poirot.

'What kind of help?'

Poirot did not speak for a moment or two. Then he said:

'Help from Mr Gale. And perhaps, later, help from you also.'

'What can I do?' asked Norman.

Poirot shot a sideways glance at him.

'You will not like it,' he said warningly.

'What is it?' repeated the young man impatiently.

Very delicately, so as not to offend English susceptibilities, Poirot used a toothpick. Then he said: 'Frankly, what I need is a blackmailer.'

'A blackmailer?' exclaimed Norman. He stared at Poirot as a man does who cannot believe his ears.

Poirot nodded.

'Precisely,' he said. 'A blackmailer.'

'But what for?'

'*Parbleu!* To blackmail.'

'Yes, but I mean who? Why?'

'Why,' said Poirot, 'is my business. As to *whom* –' He paused for a moment, then went on in a calm business-like tone:

'Here is the plan I will outline for you. You will write a note – that is to say, *I* will write a note and *you* will copy it – to the Countess of Horbury. You will mark it "Personal". In the note you will ask for an interview. You will recall yourself to her memory as having travelled to England by air on a certain occasion. You will also refer to certain business dealings of Madame Giselle's having passed into your hands.'

'And then?'

'And then you will be accorded an interview. You will go and you will say certain things (in which I will instruct you). You will ask for – let me see – ten thousand pounds.'

'You're mad!'

'Not at all,' said Poirot. 'I am eccentric, possibly, but mad, no.'

'And suppose Lady Horbury sends for the police? I shall go to prison.'

'She will not send for the police.'

'You can't *know* that.'

'*Mon cher*, practically speaking, I know everything.'

'And, anyway, I don't like it.'

'You will not get the ten thousand pounds – if that makes your conscience any clearer,' said Poirot with a twinkle.

'Yes, but look here, M. Poirot – this is the sort of wildcat scheme that might ruin me for life.'

'Ta – ta – ta – the lady will not go to the police – that I assure you.'

'She may tell her husband.'

'She will not tell her husband.'

'I don't like it.'

'Do you like losing your patients and ruining your career?'

'No, but –'

Poirot smiled at him kindly.

'You have the natural repugnance, yes? That is very natural. You have, too, the chivalrous spirit. But I can assure you that Lady Horbury is not worth all this fine feeling – to use your idiom she is a very nasty piece of goods.'

'All the same, she can't be a murderess.'

'Why?'

'Why? Because we should have seen her. Jane and I were sitting just opposite.'

'You have too many preconceived ideas. Me, I desire to straighten things out; and to do that I must *know*.'

'I don't like the idea of blackmailing a woman.'

'Ah, *mon Dieu* – what there is in a word! There will be no blackmail. You have only to produce a certain effect. After that, when the ground is prepared, I will step in.'

Norman said, 'If you land me in prison –'

'No, no, no, I am very well known at Scotland Yard. If anything should occur I will take the blame. But nothing will occur other than what I have prophesied.'

Norman surrendered with a sigh.

'All right. I'll do it. But I don't half like it.'

'Good. This is what you will write. Take a pencil.'

He dictated slowly.

'*Voilà*,' he said. 'Later I will instruct you as to what you are to say. Tell me, Mademoiselle, do you ever go to the theatre?'

'Yes, fairly often,' said Jane.

'Good. Have you seen, for instance, a play called *Down Under*?'

'Yes. I saw it about a month ago. It's rather good.'

'An American play, is it not?'

'Yes.'

'Do you remember the part of Harry, played by Mr Raymond Barraclough?'

'Yes. He was very good.'

'You thought him attractive? Yes?'

'Frightfully attractive.'

'Ah, *il est sex appeal*?'

'Decidedly,' said Jane, laughing.

'Just that – or is he a good actor as well?'

'Oh, I think he acts well too.'

'I must go and see him,' said Poirot.

Jane stared at him, puzzled.

What an odd little man he was – hopping from subject to subject like a bird from one branch to another!

Perhaps he read her thoughts. He smiled:

'You do not approve of me, Mademoiselle? Of my methods?'

'You jump about a good deal.'

'Not really. I pursue my course logically with order and method. One must not jump wildly to a conclusion. One must *eliminate*.'

'Eliminate?' said Jane. 'Is that what you're doing?' She thought a moment. 'I see. You've eliminated Mr Clancy –'

'Perhaps,' said Poirot.

'And you've eliminated us; and now you're going, perhaps, to eliminate Lady Horbury. Oh!'

She stopped as a sudden thought struck her.

'What is it, Mademoiselle?'

'That talk of attempted murder? Was that a *test*?'

'You are very quick, Mademoiselle. Yes, that was part of the course I pursue. I mention attempted murder and I watch Mr Clancy, I watch you, I watch Mr Gale – and in neither of you three is there any sign – not so much as the flicker of an eyelash. And let me tell you that I could not be

152

deceived on that point. A murderer can be ready to meet any attack that he *foresees*. But that entry in a little notebook could not have been known to any of you. So, you see, I am satisfied.'

'What a horrible, tricky sort of person you are, M. Poirot,' said Jane, rising. 'I shall never know why you are saying things.'

'That is quite simple. I want to find out things.'

'I suppose you've got very clever ways of finding out things?'

'There is only one really simple way.'

'What is that?'

'To let people tell you.'

Jane laughed.

'Suppose they don't want to?'

'Everyone likes talking about themselves.'

'I suppose they do,' admitted Jane.

'That is how many a quack makes a fortune. He encourages patients to come and sit and tell him things. How they fell out of the perambulator when they were two, and how their mother ate a pear and the juice fell on her orange dress, and how when they were one and a half they pulled their father's beard; and then he tells them that now they will not suffer from the insomnia any longer, and he takes two guineas; and they go away, having enjoyed themselves – oh, so much – and perhaps they do sleep.'

'How ridiculous,' said Jane.

'No, it is not so ridiculous as you think. It is based on a fundamental need of human nature – the need to talk – to reveal oneself. You yourself, Mademoiselle, do you not like to dwell on your childhood memories – on your mother and your father?'

'That doesn't apply in my case. I was brought up in an orphanage.'

'Ah, that is different. It is not gay, that.'

'I don't mean that we were the kind of charity orphans

who go out in scarlet bonnets and cloaks. It was quite fun really.'

'It was in England?'

'No, in Ireland – near Dublin.'

'So you are Irish. That is why you have the dark hair and the blue-grey eyes, with the look –'

'As though they had been put in with a smutty finger –' Norman finished with amusement.

'*Comment?* What is that you say?'

'That is a saying about Irish eyes – that they have been put in with a smutty finger.'

'Really? It is not elegant, that. And yet – it expresses it well.' He bowed to Jane. 'The effect is very good, Mademoiselle.'

Jane laughed as she got up.

'You'll turn my head, M. Poirot. Good night, and thank you for supper. You'll have to stand me another if Norman is sent to prison for blackmail.'

A frown came over Norman's face at the reminder.

Poirot bade the two young people good night.

When he got home he unlocked a drawer and took out a list of eleven names.

Against four of these names he put a light tick. Then he nodded his head thoughtfully.

'I think I know,' he murmured to himself. 'But I have got to be sure. *Il faut continuer.*'

CHAPTER 17

In Wandsworth

Mr Henry Mitchell was just sitting down to a supper of sausage and mash when a visitor called to see him.

Somewhat to the steward's astonishment the visitor in question was the full-moustached gentleman who had been one of the passengers on the fatal plane.

M. Poirot was very affable, very agreeable in his manner. He insisted on Mr Mitchell's getting on with his supper, paid a graceful compliment to Mrs Mitchell, who was standing staring at him open-mouthed.

He accepted a chair, remarked that it was very warm for the time of year and then gently came round to the purpose of his call.

'Scotland Yard, I fear, is not making much progress with the case,' he said.

Mitchell shook his head.

'It was an amazing business, sir – amazing. I don't see what they've got to go on. Why, if none of the people on the plane saw anything, it's going to be difficult for anyone afterwards.'

'Truly, as you say.'

'Terribly worried, Henry's been, over it,' put in his wife. 'Not able to sleep of nights.'

The steward explained:

'It's lain on my mind, sir, something terrible. The company have been very fair about it. I must say I was afraid at first I might lose my job –'

'Henry, they couldn't. It would have been cruelly unfair.'

His wife sounded highly indignant. She was a buxom, highly-complexioned woman with snapping dark eyes.

'Things don't always happen fairly, Ruth. Still it turned

out better than I thought. They absolve me from blame. But I felt it, if you understand me. I was in charge, as it were.'

'I understand your feelings,' said Poirot sympathetically. 'But I assure you that you are over-conscientious. Nothing that happened was your fault.'

'That's what *I* say, sir,' put in Mrs Mitchell.

Mitchell shook his head.

'I ought to have noticed that the lady was dead sooner. If I'd tried to wake her up when I first took round the bills –'

'It would have made little difference. Death, they think, was very nearly instantaneous.'

'He worries so,' said Mrs Mitchell. 'I tell him not to bother his head so. Who's to know what reason foreigners have for murdering each other; and if you ask me, I think it's a dirty trick to have done it in a British aeroplane.'

She finished her sentence with an indignant and patriotic snort.

Mitchell shook his head in a puzzled way.

'It weighs on me, so to speak. Every time I go on duty I'm in a state. And then the gentleman from Scotland Yard asking me again and again if nothing unusual or sudden occurred on the way over. Makes me feel as though I *must* have forgotten something – and yet I know I haven't. It was a most uneventful voyage in every way until – until *it* happened.'

'Blowpipes and darts – heathen, I call it,' said Mrs Mitchell.

'You are right,' said Poirot, addressing her with a flattering air of being struck by her remarks. 'Not so is an English murder committed.'

'You're right, sir.'

'You know, Mrs Mitchell, I can almost guess what part of England you come from.'

'Dorset, sir. Not far from Bridport. That's my home.'

'Exactly,' said Poirot. 'A lovely part of the world.'

'It is that. London isn't a patch on Dorset. My folk have

been settled in Dorset for over two hundred years – and I've got Dorset in the blood, as you might say.'

'Yes, indeed.' He turned to the steward again. 'There's one thing I'd like to ask you, Mitchell.'

The man's brow contracted.

'I've told you all that I know – indeed I have, sir.'

'Yes, yes – this is a very trifling matter. I only wondered if anything on the table – Madame Giselle's table, I mean – was disarranged?'

'You mean when – when I found her?'

'Yes. The spoons and forks – the salt cellar – anything like that.'

The man shook his head.

'There wasn't anything of that kind on the tables. Everything was cleared away bar the coffee cups. I didn't notice anything myself. I shouldn't, though. I was much too flustered. But the police would know that, sir, they searched the plane through and through.'

'Ah, well,' said Poirot. 'It is no matter. Sometime I must have a word with your colleague – Davis.'

'He's on the early 8.45 am service now, sir.'

'Has this business upset him much?'

'Oh, well, sir, you see he's only a young fellow. If you ask me, he's almost enjoyed it all. The excitement, and everyone standing him drinks and wanting to hear about it.'

'Has he perhaps a young lady?' asked Poirot. 'Doubtless his connexion with the crime would be very thrilling to her.'

'He's courting old Johnson's daughter at the Crown and Feathers,' said Mrs Mitchell. 'But she's a sensible girl – got her head screwed on the right way. She doesn't approve of being mixed up with a murder.'

'A very sound point of view,' said Poirot, rising. 'Well, thank you, Mr Mitchell – and you, Mrs Mitchell – and I beg of you, my friend, do not let this weigh upon your mind.'

When he had departed Mitchell said, 'The thick heads in the jury at the inquest thought he'd done it. But if you ask me, he's secret service.'

'If you ask me,' said Mrs Mitchell, 'there's Bolshies at the back of it.'

Poirot had said that he must have a word with the other steward, Davis, sometime. As a matter of fact he had it not many hours later, in the bar of the Crown and Feathers.

He asked Davis the same question he had asked Mitchell.

'Nothing disarranged – no, sir. You mean upset? That kind of thing?'

'I mean – well, shall we say something missing from the table – or something that would not usually be there –'

Davis said slowly:

'There was *something* – I noticed it when I was clearing up, after the police had done with the place – but I don't suppose that it's the sort of thing you mean. It's only that the dead lady had two coffee spoons in her saucer. It does sometimes happen when we're serving in a hurry. I noticed it because there's a superstition about that; they say two spoons in a saucer means a wedding.'

'Was there a spoon missing from anyone else's saucer?'

'No, sir, not that I noticed. Mitchell or I must have taken the cup and saucer along that way – as I say one does sometimes what with the hurry and all. I laid two sets of fish knives and forks only a week ago. On the whole it's better than laying the table short, for then you have to interrupt yourself and go and fetch the extra knife, or whatever it is you've forgotten.'

Poirot asked one more question – a somewhat jocular one:

'What do you think of French girls, Davis?'

'English are good enough for me, sir.'

And he grinned at a plump, fair-haired girl behind the bar.

CHAPTER 18

In Queen Victoria Street

Mr James Ryder was rather surprised when a card bearing the name of M. Hercule Poirot was brought to him.

He knew that the name was familiar, but for the moment he could not remember why. Then he said to himself:

'Oh, *that* fellow!' and told the clerk to show the visitor in.

M. Hercule Poirot was looking very jaunty. In one hand he carried a cane, he had a flower in his buttonhole.

'You will forgive my troubling you, I trust,' said Poirot. 'It is this affair of the death of Madame Giselle.'

'Yes?' said Mr Ryder. 'Well, what about it? Sit down, won't you? Have a cigar?'

'I thank you, no. I smoke my own cigarettes. Perhaps you will accept one?'

Ryder regarded Poirot's tiny cigarettes with a somewhat dubious eye.

'Think I'll have one of my own, if it's all the same to you. Might swallow one of those by mistake.' He laughed heartily.

'The inspector was round here a few days ago,' said Mr Ryder when he had induced his lighter to work. 'Nosey, that's what those fellows are. Can't mind their own business.'

'They have, I suppose, to get information,' said Poirot mildly.

'They needn't be so damned offensive about it,' said Mr Ryder bitterly. 'A man's got his feelings – and his business reputation to think about.'

'You are, perhaps, a little over-sensitive.'

'I'm in a delicate position, I am,' said Mr Ryder. 'Sitting where I did, just in front of her – well, it looks fishy, I suppose. I can't help where I sat. If I'd known that woman was going to be murdered I wouldn't have come by that plane at all. I don't know, though, perhaps I would.'

159

He looked thoughtful for a moment.

'Has good come out of evil?' asked Poirot, smiling.

'It's funny your saying that. It has, and it hasn't, in a manner of speaking. I mean I've had a lot of worry. I've been badgered. Things have been insinuated. And why *me*? that's what I say. Why don't they go and worry that Dr Hubbard – Bryant, I mean. Doctors are the people who can get hold of high-falutin' undetectable poisons. How'd I get hold of snake juice? I ask you!'

'You were saying,' said Poirot, 'that although you had been put to a lot of inconvenience –?'

'Ah, yes, there was a bright side to the picture. I don't mind telling you I cleaned up a tidy little sum from the papers. Eyewitness stuff – though there was more of the reporter's imagination than of my eyesight; but that's neither here nor there.'

'It is interesting,' said Poirot, 'how a crime affects the lives of people who are quite outside it. Take yourself, for example – you make suddenly a quite unexpected sum of money – a sum of money perhaps particularly welcome at the moment.'

'Money's always welcome,' said Mr Ryder.

He eyed Poirot sharply.

'Sometimes the need of it is imperative. For that reason men embezzle – they make fraudulent entries –' He waved his hands. 'All sorts of complications arise.'

'Well, don't let's get gloomy about it,' said Mr Ryder.

'True. Why dwell on the dark side of the picture? This money was grateful to you – since you failed to raise a loan in Paris –'

'How the devil did you know that?' asked Mr Ryder angrily.

Hercule Poirot smiled.

'At any rate it is true.'

'It's true enough, but I don't particularly want it to get about.'

'I will be discretion itself, I assure you.'

'It's odd,' mused Mr Ryder, 'how small a sum will sometimes put a man in Queer Street. Just a small sum of ready money to tide him over a crisis – and if he can't get hold of that infinitesimal sum, to hell with his credit. Yes, it's damned odd. Money's odd. Credit's odd. Come to that, life is odd!'

'Very true.'

'By the way, what was it you wanted to see me about?'

'It is a little delicate. It has come to my ears – in the course of my profession, you understand – that in spite of your denials you *did* have dealings with this woman Giselle.'

'Who says so? It's a lie! I never saw the woman.'

'Dear me, that is very curious!'

'Curious! It's damned libel.'

Poirot looked at him thoughtfully.

'Ah,' he said, 'I must look into the matter.'

'What do you mean? What are you getting at?'

Poirot shook his head.

'Do not enrage yourself; there must be – a mistake.'

'I should think there was. Catch me getting myself mixed up with these high-toned Society moneylenders. Society woman with gambling debts – that's their sort.'

Poirot rose.

'I must apologize for having been misinformed.' He paused at the door. 'By the way, just as a matter of curiosity, what made you call Dr Bryant Dr *Hubbard* just now?'

'Blessed if I know. Let me see – Oh, yes, I think it must have been the flute. The nursery rhyme, you know. Old Mother Hubbard's dog – *But when she came back he was playing the flute*. Odd thing how you mix up names.'

'Ah, yes, the flute . . . These things interest me, you understand, psychologically.'

Mr Ryder snorted at the word psychologically. It savoured to him of what he called that tom-fool business psychoanalysis.

He looked at Poirot with suspicion.

CHAPTER 19

Enter and Exit Mr Robinson

The Countess of Horbury sat in her bedroom at 315 Grosvenor Square in front of her toilet table. Gold brushes and boxes, jars of face cream, boxes of powder – dainty luxury all around her. But in the midst of the luxury Cicely Horbury sat with dry lips and a face on which the rouge showed up in unbecoming patches on her cheeks.

She read the letter for the fourth time.

'The Countess of Horbury.

'DEAR MADAM,

　　　　re Madame Giselle, deceased.

I am the holder of certain documents formerly in the possession of the deceased lady. If you or Mr Raymond Barraclough are interested in the matter, I should be happy to call upon you with a view to discussing the affair.

'Or perhaps you would prefer me to deal with your husband in the matter?

'Yours truly,
'JOHN ROBINSON.'

Stupid, to read the same thing over and over again . . .

As though the words might alter their meaning.

She picked up the envelope – two envelopes, the first with 'Personal' on it, the second with 'Private and Very Confidential.'

'Private and Very Confidential . . .'

The beast . . . the beast . . .

And that lying old Frenchwoman, who had sworn that 'all

arrangements were made to protect clients in case of her own sudden demise . . .'

Damn her . . . Life was hell – hell . . .

'Oh God, my nerves,' thought Cicely. 'It isn't fair. It isn't fair . . .'

Her shaking hand went out to a gold-topped bottle . . .

'It will steady me, pull me together . . .'

She snuffed the stuff up her nose.

There. Now she could think! What to do? See the man, of course. Though where she could raise any money – perhaps a lucky flutter at that place in Carlos Street . . .

But time enough to think of that later. See the man – find out what he knows.

She went over to the writing-table, dashed off in her big, unformed handwriting:

The Countess of Horbury presents her compliments to Mr John Robinson and will see him if he calls at eleven o'clock tomorrow morning . . .

'Will I do?' asked Norman.

He flushed a little under Poirot's startled gaze.

'Name of a name,' said Hercule Poirot. 'What kind of a comedy is it that you are playing?'

Norman Gale flushed even more deeply.

He mumbled, 'You said a slight disguise would be as well.'

Poirot sighed, then he took the young man by the arm and marched him to the looking-glass.

'Regard yourself,' he said. 'That is all I ask of you – regard yourself! What do you think you are – a Santa Claus dressed up to amuse the children? I agree that your beard is not white: no, it is black – the colour for villains. But what a beard – a beard that screams to Heaven! A cheap beard, my friend, and most imperfectly and amateurishly attached! Then there are your eyebrows. But it is that you have the mania for false hair? The spirit gum one smells it several yards away; and if you think that anyone will fail to perceive that you have a piece of sticking plaster attached to a tooth, you are mistaken. My friend, it is not your *métier* – decidedly not – to play the part.'

'I acted in amateur theatricals a good deal at one time,' said Norman Gale stiffly.

'I can hardly believe it. At any rate, I presume they did not let you indulge in your own ideas of makeup. Even behind the footlights your appearance would be singularly unconvincing. In Grosvenor Square in broad daylight –'

Poirot gave an eloquent shrug of the shoulders by way of finishing the sentence.

'No, *mon ami*,' he said. 'You are a blackmailer, not a comedian. I want her ladyship to fear you – not to die of laughing when she sees you. I observe that I wound you by what I am saying. I regret, but it is a moment when only the truth will serve. Take this and this –' He pressed various jars upon him. 'Go into the bathroom and let us have an end of what you call in this country the fooltommery.'

Crushed, Norman Gale obeyed. When he emerged a quarter of an hour later, his face a vivid shade of brick red, Poirot gave him a nod of approval.

'*Très bien*. The farce is over. The serious business begins. I will permit you to have a small moustache. But I will, if you please, attach it to you myself. There – and now we will part the hair differently – so. That is quite enough. Now let me see if you at least know your lines.'

He listened with attention, then nodded.

'That is good. *En avant* – and good luck to you.'

'I devoutly hope so. I shall probably find an enraged husband and a couple of policemen.'

Poirot reassured him.

'Have no anxiety. All will march to a marvel.'

'So you say,' muttered Norman rebelliously.

With his spirits at zero, he departed on his distasteful mission.

At Grosvenor Square he was shown into a small room on the first floor. There, after a minute or two, Lady Horbury came to him.

Norman braced himself. He must not – positively must not – show that he was new to this business.

'Mr Robinson?' said Cicely.

'At your service,' said Norman, and bowed.

'Damn it all – just like a shop-walker,' he thought disgustedly. 'That's fright.'

'I had your letter,' said Cicely.

Norman pulled himself together. 'The old fool said I couldn't act,' he said to himself with a mental grin.

Aloud he said rather insolently:

'Quite so – well, what about it, Lady Horbury?'

'I don't know what you mean.'

'Come, come. Must we really go into details? Everyone knows how pleasant a – well, call it a weekend at the seaside – can be; but husbands seldom agree. I think you know, Lady Horbury, just exactly what the evidence consists of. Wonderful woman, old Giselle. Always had the goods. Hotel evidence, etc., is quite first class. Now the question is who wants it most – you or Lord Horbury? That's the question.'

She stood there quivering.

'I'm a seller,' said Norman, his voice growing commoner as he threw himself more whole-heartedly into the part of Mr Robinson. 'Are you a buyer? That's the question.'

'How did you get hold of this – evidence?'

'Now really, Lady Horbury, that's rather beside the point. I've got it, that's the main thing.'

'I don't believe you. Show it to me.'

'Oh, no.' Norman shook his head with a cunning leer. 'I didn't bring anything with me. I'm not so green as that. If we agree to do business, that's another matter. I'll show you the stuff before you hand the money over. All fair and above-board.'

'How – how much?'

'Ten thousand of the best – pounds, not dollars.'

'Impossible. I could never lay my hands on anything like that amount.'

'It's wonderful what you can do if you try. Jewels aren't fetching what they did, but pearls are still pearls. Look here, to oblige a lady I'll make it eight thousand. That's my last word. And I'll give you two days to think it over.'

'I can't get the money, I tell you.'

Norman sighed and shook his head.

'Well, perhaps it's only right Lord Horbury should know what's been going on. I believe I'm correct in saying that a divorced woman gets no alimony – and Mr Barraclough's a very promising young actor, but he's not touching big money. Now not another word. I'll leave you to think it over; and mind what I say – I mean it.'

He paused and then added:

'I mean it, just as Giselle meant it . . .'

Then quickly, before the wretched woman could reply, he had left the room.

'Ouch!' said Norman as he reached the street. He wiped his brow. 'Thank goodness *that's* over.'

It was a bare hour later when a card was brought to Lady Horbury.

'M. Hercule Poirot.'

She thrust it aside. 'Who is he? I can't see him!'

'He said, m'lady, that he was here at the request of Mr Raymond Barraclough.'

'Oh.' She paused. 'Very well, show him in.'

The butler departed, reappeared.

'M. Hercule Poirot.'

Exquisitely dressed in the most dandiacal style, M. Poirot entered, bowed.

The butler closed the door. Cicely took a step forward.

'Mr Barraclough sent you –?'

'Sit down, Madame.' His tone was kindly but authoritative.

Mechanically she sat. He took a chair near her. His manner was fatherly and reassuring.

'Madame, I entreat you, look upon me as a friend. I come to advise you. You are, I know, in grave trouble.'

She murmured faintly, 'I don't –'

'*Ecoutez*, Madame, I do not ask you to give away your secrets. It is unnecessary. I know them beforehand. That is the essence of being a good detective – to know.'

'A detective?' Her eyes widened. 'I remember – you were on the plane. It was you –'

'Precisely, it was me. Now, Madame, let us get to business. As I said just now, I do not press you to confide in me. You shall not start by telling *me* things. *I* will tell to *you*. This morning, not an hour ago, you had a visitor. That visitor – his name was Brown, perhaps?'

'Robinson,' said Cicely faintly.

'It is the same thing – Brown, Smith, Robinson – he uses them in turn. He came here to blackmail you, Madame. He has in his possession certain proofs of – shall we say – indiscretion? Those proofs were once in the keeping of Madame Giselle. Now this man has them. He offers them to you for, perhaps, seven thousand pounds.'

'Eight.'

'Eight, then. And you, Madame, will not find it easy to get that sum very quickly?'

'I can't do it – I simply can't do it . . . I'm in debt already. I don't know what to do . . .'

'Calm yourself, Madame. I come to assist you.'

She stared at him.

'How do you know all this?'

'Simply, Madame, because I am Hercule Poirot. *Eh bien*, have no fears – place yourself in my hands – I will deal with this Mr Robinson.'

'Yes,' said Cicely sharply. 'And how much will you want?'

Hercule Poirot bowed.

'I shall ask only a photograph, signed, of a very beautiful lady . . .'

She cried out, 'Oh, dear, I don't know what to do . . . My nerves . . . I'm going mad.'

'No, no, all is well. Trust Hercule Poirot. Only, Madame, I must have the truth – the whole truth – do not keep anything back or my hands will be tied.'

'And you'll get me out of this mess?'

'I swear to you solemnly that you will never hear of Mr Robinson again.'

She said, 'All right. I'll tell you everything.'

'Good. Now then, you borrowed money from this woman Giselle?'

Lady Horbury nodded.

'When was that? When did it begin, I mean?'

'Eighteen months ago. I was in a hole.'

'Gambling?'

'Yes. I had an appalling run of luck.'

'And she lent you as much as you wanted?'

'Not at first. Only a small sum to begin with.'

'Who sent you to her?'

'Raymond – Mr Barraclough told me that he had heard she lent money to Society women.'

'But later she lent you more?'

'Yes – as much as I wanted. It seemed like a miracle at the time.'

'It was Madame Giselle's special kind of miracle,' said Poirot drily. 'I gather that before then you and Mr Barraclough had become – er – friends?'

'Yes.'

'But you were very anxious that your husband should not know about it?'

Cicely cried angrily, 'Stephen's a prig. He's tired of me. He wants to marry someone else. He'd have jumped at the thought of divorcing me.'

'And you did not want – divorce?'

'No. I – I –'

'You liked your position – and also you enjoyed the use of a very ample income. Quite so. *Les femmes*, naturally, they must look after themselves. To proceed – there arose the question of repayment?'

'Yes, and I – I couldn't pay back the money. And then the old devil turned nasty. She knew about me and Raymond. She'd found out places and dates and everything – I can't think how.'

'She had her methods,' said Poirot drily. 'And she threatened, I suppose, to send all this evidence to Lord Horbury?'

'Yes, unless I paid up.'

'And you couldn't pay?'

'No.'

'So her death was quite providential?'

Cicely Horbury said earnestly, 'It seemed too, too wonderful.'

'Ah, precisely – too, too wonderful. But it made you a little nervous, perhaps?'

'Nervous?'

'Well, after all, Madame, you alone of anyone on the plane had a motive for desiring her death.'

She drew in her breath sharply.

'I know. It was awful. I was in an absolute state about it.'

'Especially since you had been to see her in Paris the night before, and had had something of a scene with her?'

'The old devil! She wouldn't budge an inch. I think she actually enjoyed it. Oh, she was a beast through and through! I came away like a rag.'

'And yet you said at the inquest that you had never seen the woman before?'

'Well, naturally, what else could I say?'

Poirot looked at her thoughtfully.

'*You*, Madame, could say nothing else.'

'It's been too ghastly – nothing but lies – lies – lies. That dreadful inspector man has been here again and again badgering me with questions. But I felt pretty safe. I could see he was only trying it on. He didn't know anything.'

'If one does guess, one should guess with assurance.'

'And then,' continued Cicely, pursuing her own line of thought, 'I couldn't help feeling that if anything *were* to leak out, it would have leaked out at once. I felt safe – till that awful letter yesterday.'

'You have not been afraid all this time?'

'Of course I've been afraid!'

'But of what? Of exposure, or of being arrested for murder?'

The colour ebbed away from her cheeks.

'Murder – but I didn't – Oh, you don't believe *that*! I didn't kill her. I didn't!'

'You wanted her dead . . .'

'Yes, but I didn't kill her . . . Oh, you must believe me – you must. I never moved from my seat. I –'

She broke off. Her beautiful blue eyes were fixed on him imploringly.

Hercule Poirot nodded soothingly.

'I believe you, Madame, for two reasons – first, because of your sex, and secondly because of – a wasp.'

She stared at him.

'A wasp?'

'Exactly. That does not make sense to you, I see. Now, then, let us attend to the matter in hand. I will deal with this Mr Robinson. I pledge you my word that you shall never see or hear of him again. I will settle his – his – I have forgotten the word – his bacon? No, his goat. Now in return for my services I will ask you two little questions. Was Mr Barraclough in Paris the day before the murder?'

'Yes, we dined together. But he thought it better I should go and see the woman alone.'

'Ah, he did, did he? Now, Madame, one further

question: Your stage name before you were married was Cicely Bland. Was that your real name?'

'No, my real name is Martha Jebb. But the other –'

'Made a better professional name. And you were born – where?'

'Doncaster. But why –'

'Mere curiosity. Forgive me. And now, Lady Horbury, will you permit me to give you some advice? Why not arrange with your husband a discreet divorce?'

'And let him marry that woman?'

'And let him marry that woman. You have a generous heart, Madame; and besides, you will be safe – oh, so safe – and your husband he will pay you an income.'

'Not a very large one.'

'*Eh bien*, once you are free you will marry a millionaire.'

'There aren't any nowadays.'

'Ah, do not believe that, Madame. The man who had three millions perhaps now he has two millions – *eh bien*, it is still enough.'

Cicely laughed.

'You're very persuasive, M. Poirot. And are you really sure that dreadful man will never bother me again?'

'On the word of Hercule Poirot,' said that gentleman solemnly.

CHAPTER 20

In Harley Street

Detective-Inspector Japp walked briskly up Harley Street and stopped at a certain door.

He asked for Dr Bryant.

'Have you an appointment, sir?'

'No, I'll just write a few words.'

On an official card he wrote:

'Should be much obliged if you could spare me a few moments. I won't keep you long.'

He sealed up the card in an envelope and gave it to the butler.

He was shown into a waiting-room. There were two women there and a man. Japp settled down with an elderly copy of *Punch*.

The butler reappeared and crossing the floor, said in a discreet voice:

'If you wouldn't mind waiting a short time, sir, the doctor will see you, but he's very busy this morning.'

Japp nodded. He did not in the least mind waiting – in fact he rather welcomed it. The two women had begun to talk. They had obviously a very high opinion of Dr Bryant's abilities. More patients came in. Evidently Dr Bryant was doing well in his profession.

'Fairly coining money,' thought Japp to himself. 'That doesn't look like needing to borrow; but of course the loan may have taken place a long time ago. Anyway, he's got a fine practice; a breath of scandal would burst it to bits. That's the worst of being a doctor.'

Quarter of an hour later the butler reappeared and said:

'The doctor will see you now, sir.'

Japp was shown into Dr Bryant's consulting-room – a room at the back of the house with a big window. The doctor was sitting at his desk. He rose and shook hands with the detective.

His fine-lined face showed fatigue, but he seemed in no way disturbed by the inspector's visit.

'What can I do for you, Inspector?' he said as he resumed his seat and motioned Japp to a chair opposite.

'I must apologize first for calling in your consulting hours, but I shan't keep you long, sir.'

'That is all right, I suppose it is about the aeroplane death?'

'Quite right, sir. We're still working on it.'

'With any result?'

'We're not as far on as we'd like to be. I really came to ask you some questions about the method employed. It's this snake venom business that I can't get the hang of.'

'I'm not a toxicologist, you know,' said Dr Bryant, smiling. 'Such things aren't in my line. Winterspoon's your man.'

'Ah, but you see, it's like this, Doctor. Winterspoon's an expert – and you know what experts are. They talk so that the ordinary man can't understand them. But as far as I can make out there's a medical side to this business. Is it true that snake venom is sometimes injected for epilepsy?'

'I'm not a specialist in epilepsy, either,' said Dr Bryant. 'But I believe that injections of cobra venom have been used in the treatment of epilepsy with excellent results. But, as I say, that's not really my line of country.'

'I know – I know. What it really amounts to is this: I felt that you'd take an interest, having been on the aeroplane yourself. I thought it possible that you'd have some ideas on the subject yourself that might be useful to me. It's not much good my going to an expert if I don't know what to ask him.'

Dr Bryant smiled.

'There is something in what you say, Inspector. There is probably no man living who can remain entirely unaffected by having come in close contact with murder . . . I am interested, I admit. I have speculated a good deal about the case in my quiet way.'

'And what do you think, sir?'

Bryant shook his head slowly.

'It amazes me – the whole thing seems almost – unreal – if I might put it that way. An astounding way of committing a crime. It seems a chance in a hundred that the murderer was not seen. He must be a person with a reckless disregard of risks.'

'Very true, sir.'

'The choice of poison is equally amazing. How could a would-be murderer possibly get hold of such a thing?'

'I know. It seems incredible. Why, I don't suppose one man in a thousand has ever heard of such a thing as a boomslang, much less actually handled the venom. You yourself, sir, now, you're a doctor – but I don't suppose you've ever handled the stuff.'

'There are certainly not many opportunities of doing so. I have a friend who works at tropical research. In his laboratory there are various specimens of dried snake venoms – that of the cobra, for instance – but I cannot remember any specimen of the boomslang.'

'Perhaps you can help me –' Japp took out a piece of paper and handed it to the doctor. 'Winterspoon wrote down these three names – said I might get information there. Do you know any of these men?'

'I know Professor Kennedy slightly. Heidler I know well; mention my name and I'm sure he'll do all he can for you. Carmichael's an Edinburgh man – I don't know him personally – but I believe they've done some good work up there.'

'Thank you, sir, I'm much obliged. Well, I won't keep you any longer.'

When Japp emerged into Harley Street he was smiling to himself in a pleased fashion.

'Nothing like tact,' he said to himself. 'Tact does it. I'll be bound he never saw what I was after. Well, that's that.'

CHAPTER 21

The Three Clues

When Japp got back to Scotland Yard he was told that M. Hercule Poirot was waiting to see him.

Japp greeted his friend heartily.

'Well, M. Poirot, and what brings you along. Any news?'

'I came to ask you for news, my good Japp.'

'If that isn't just like you. Well, there isn't much and that's the truth. The dealer fellow in Paris has identified the blowpipe all right. Fournier's been worrying the life out of me from Paris about his *moment psychologique*. I've questioned those stewards till I'm blue in the face, and they stick to it that there wasn't a *moment psychologique*. Nothing startling or out of the way happened on the voyage.'

'It might have occurred when they were both in the front car.'

'I've questioned the passengers, too. Everyone can't be lying.'

'In one case I investigated everyone was!'

'You and your cases! To tell the truth, M. Poirot, I'm not very happy. The more I look into things the less I get. The Chief's inclined to look on me rather coldly. But what can I do? Luckily it's one of those semi-foreign cases. We can put it on the Frenchmen over here – and in Paris they say it was done by an Englishman and that it's our business.'

'Do you really believe the Frenchmen did it?'

'Well, frankly, I don't. As I look at it an archaeologist is a poor kind of fish. Always burrowing in the ground and talking through his hat about what happened thousands of years ago – and how do they know, I should like to know? Who's to contradict them? They say some rotten string of beads is five thousand three hundred and twenty-two years

175

old, and who's to say it isn't? Well, there they are – liars, perhaps – though they seem to believe it themselves – but harmless. I had an old chap in here the other day who'd had a scarab pinched – terrible state he was in – nice old boy, but helpless as a baby in arms. No, between you and me, I don't think for a minute that pair of French archaeologists did it.'

'Who *do* you think did it?'

'Well – there's Clancy, of course. He's in a queer way. Goes about muttering to himself. He's got something on his mind.'

'The plot of a new book, perhaps.'

'It may be that – and it may be something else; but, try as I may, I can't get a line on motive. I still think CL 52 in the black book is Lady Horbury; but I can't get anything out of her. She's pretty hard-boiled, I can tell you.'

Poirot smiled to himself. Japp went on:

'The stewards – well, I can't find a thing to connect them with Giselle.'

'Dr Bryant?'

'I think I'm on to something there. Rumours about him and a patient. Pretty woman – nasty husband – takes drugs or something. If he's not careful he'll be struck off the medical council. That fits in with RT 362 well enough, and I don't mind telling you that I've got a pretty shrewd idea where he could have got the snake venom from. I went to see him and he gave himself away rather badly over that. Still, so far it is all surmise – no *facts*. Facts aren't any too easy to get at in this case. Ryder seems all square and above board – says he went to raise a loan in Paris and couldn't get it – gave names and addresses – all checked up. I've found out that the firm was nearly in Queer Street about a week or two ago, but they seem to be just pulling through. There you are again – unsatisfactory. The whole thing is a muddle.'

'There is no such thing as muddle – obscurity, yes – but muddle can exist only in a disorderly brain.'

'Use any word you choose. The result's the same. Fournier's stumped, too. I suppose you've got it all taped out, but you'd rather not tell!'

'You mock yourself at me. I have not got it all taped out. I proceed a step at a time, with order and method, but there is still far to go.'

'I can't help feeling glad to hear that. Let's hear about these orderly steps.'

Poirot smiled.

'I make a little table – so.' He took a paper from his pocket. 'My idea is this: A murder is an action performed to bring about a certain result.'

'Say that again slowly.'

'It is not difficult.'

'Probably not – but you make it sound so.'

'No, no, it is very simple. Say you want money – you get it when an aunt dies. *Bien* – you perform an action – this is to kill the aunt – and get the result – inherit the money.'

'I wish I had some aunts like that,' sighed Japp. 'Go ahead, I see your idea. You mean there's *got* to be a motive.'

'I prefer my own way of putting it. An action is performed – the action being murder – what now are the results of that action? By studying the different results we should get the answer to our conundrum. The results of a single action may be very varied – that particular action affects a lot of different people. *Eh bien*, I study today – three weeks after the crime – the result in eleven different cases.'

He spread out the paper.

Japp leaned forward with some interest and read over Poirot's shoulder:

Miss Grey. Result – temporary improvement. Increased salary.

Mr Gale. Result – bad. Loss of practice.

Lady Horbury. Result good, if she's CL 52.

Miss Kerr. Result – bad, since Giselle's death makes it

more unlikely Lord Horbury will get the evidence to divorce his wife.

'H'm.' Japp interrupted his scrutiny. 'So you think she's keen on his lordship? You are a one for nosing out love affairs.'

Poirot smiled. Japp bent over the chart once more.

Mr Clancy. Result – good – expects to make money by book dealing with the murder.
Dr Bryant. Result – good if RT 362.
Mr Ryder. Result – good, owing to small amount of cash obtained through articles on murder which tided firm over delicate time. Also good if Ryder is XVB 724.
M. Dupont. Result – unaffected.
M. Jean Dupont. Result – the same.
Mitchell. Result – unaffected.
Davis. Result – unaffected.

'And you think that's going to help you?' asked Japp sceptically. 'I can't see that writing down "*I don't know. I don't know. I can't tell*," makes it any better.'

'It gives one a clear classification,' explained Poirot. 'In four cases – Mr Clancy, Miss Grey, Mr Ryder, and I think I may say Lady Horbury – there is a result on the credit side. In the cases of Mr Gale and Miss Kerr there is a result on the debit side – in four cases there is no result at all – so far as we know – and in one, Dr Bryant, there is either no result or a distinct gain.'

'And so?' asked Japp.

'And so,' said Poirot, 'we must go on seeking.'

'With precious little to go upon,' said Japp gloomily. 'The truth of it is that we're hung up until we can get what we want from Paris. It's the Giselle side that wants going into. I bet I could have got more out of that maid than Fournier did.'

'I doubt it, my friend. The most interesting thing about this case is the personality of the dead woman. A woman without friends – without relations – without, as one might *say* – any *personal* life. A woman who was once young, who once loved and suffered and then – with a firm hand pulled down the shutter – all that was over; not a photograph, not a souvenir, not a knick-knack. Marie Morisot became Madame Giselle – moneylender.'

'Do you think there is a clue in her past?'

'Perhaps.'

'Well, we could do with it! There aren't any clues in this case.'

'Oh, yes, my friend, there are.'

'The blowpipe, of course –'

'No, no, not the blowpipe.'

'Well, let's hear your ideas of the clues in the case.'

Poirot smiled.

'I will give them titles – like the names of Mr Clancy's stories: The Clue of the Wasp. The Clue in the Passenger's Baggage. The Clue of the Extra Coffee Spoon.'

'You're potty,' said Japp kindly, and added; 'What's this about a coffee spoon?'

'Madame Giselle had two spoons in her saucer.'

'That's supposed to mean a wedding.'

'In this case,' said Poirot, 'it meant a funeral.'

CHAPTER 22

Jane Takes a New Job

When Norman Gale, Jane and Poirot met for dinner on the night after the 'blackmailing incident' Norman was relieved to hear that his services as 'Mr Robinson' were no longer required.

'He is dead, the good Mr Robinson,' said Poirot. He raised his glass. 'Let us drink to his memory.'

'RIP,' said Norman with a laugh.

'What happened?' asked Jane of Poirot.

He smiled at her.

'I found out what I wanted to know.'

'Was she mixed up with Giselle?'

'Yes.'

'That was pretty clear from my interview with her,' said Norman.

'Quite so,' said Poirot. 'But I wanted a full and detailed story.'

'And you got it?'

'I got it.'

They both looked at him inquiringly, but Poirot, in a provoking manner, began to discuss the relationship between a career and life.

'There are not so many round pegs in square holes as one might think. Most people, in spite of what they tell you, choose the occupations that they secretly desire. You will hear a man say who works in an office, "I should like to explore – to rough it in far countries." But you will find that he likes reading the fiction that deals with that subject, but that he himself prefers the safety and moderate comfort of an office stool.'

'According to you,' said Jane, 'my desire for foreign

travel isn't genuine – messing about with women's heads is my true vocation – well, that *isn't* true.'

Poirot smiled at her.

'You are young still. Naturally one tries this, that and the other, but what one eventually settles down into is the life one prefers.'

'And suppose I prefer being rich?'

'Ah, that, it is more difficult!'

'I don't agree with you,' said Gale. 'I'm a dentist by chance – not choice. My uncle was a dentist – he wanted me to come in with him, but I was all for adventure and seeing the world. I chucked dentistry and went off to farm in South Africa. However, that wasn't much good – I hadn't got enough experience. I had to accept the old man's offer and come and set up business with him.'

'And now you are thinking of chucking dentistry again and going off to Canada. You have a Dominion complex!'

'This time I shall be forced to do it.'

'Ah, but it is incredible how often things force one to do the thing one would like to do.'

'Nothing's forcing me to travel,' said Jane wistfully. 'I wish it would.'

'*Eh bien*, I make you an offer here and now. I go to Paris next week. If you like you can take the job of my secretary – I will give you a good salary.'

Jane shook her head.

'I mustn't give up Antoine's. It's a good job.'

'So is mine a good job.'

'Yes, but it's only temporary.'

'I will obtain you another post of the same kind.'

'Thanks, but I don't think I'll risk it.'

Poirot looked at her and smiled enigmatically.

Three days later he was rung up.

'M. Poirot,' said Jane, 'is that job still open?'

'But yes. I go to Paris on Monday.'

'You really mean it? I can come?'

'Yes, but what has happened to make you change your mind?'

'I've had a row with Antoine. As a matter of fact I lost my temper with a customer. She was an – an absolute – well, I can't say just what she was through the telephone. I was feeling nervy and instead of doing my soothing syrup stuff I just let rip and told her exactly what I thought of her.'

'Ah, the thought of the great wide open spaces.'

'What's that you say?'

'I say that your mind was dwelling on a certain subject.'

'It wasn't my mind, it was my tongue that slipped. I enjoyed it – her eyes looked just like her beastly Pekingese's – as though they were going to drop out – but here I am – thrown out on my ear, as you might say. I must get another job sometime, I suppose – but I'd like to come to Paris first.'

'Good, it is arranged. On the way over I will give you your instructions.'

Poirot and his new secretary did not travel by air, for which Jane was secretly thankful. The unpleasant experience of her last trip had shaken her nerve. She did not want to be reminded of that lolling figure in rusty black . . .

On their way from Calais to Paris they had the compartment to themselves, and Poirot gave Jane some idea of his plans.

'There are several people in Paris that I have to see. There is the lawyer – Maître Thibault. There is also M. Fournier of the Sûreté – a melancholy man, but intelligent. And there are M. Dupont *père* and M. Dupont *fils*. Now, Mademoiselle Jane, whilst I am taking on the father I shall leave the son to you. You are very charming, very attractive – I fancy that M. Dupont will remember you from the inquest.'

'I've seen him since then,' said Jane, her colour rising slightly.

'Indeed? And how was that?'

Jane, her colour rising a little more, described their meeting in the Corner House.

'Excellent – better and better. Ah, it was a famous idea of mine to bring you to Paris with me. Now listen carefully, Mademoiselle Jane. As far as possible do not discuss the Giselle affair, but do not avoid the subject if Jean Dupont introduces it. It might be well if, without actually saying so, you could convey the impression that Lady Horbury is suspected of the crime. My reason for coming to Paris, you can say, is to confer with M. Fournier and to inquire particularly into any dealings Lady Horbury may have had with the dead woman.'

'Poor Lady Horbury – you do make her a stalking horse!'

'She is not the type I admire – *eh bien*, let her be useful for once.'

Jane hesitated for a minute, then said:

'You don't suspect young M. Dupont of the crime, do you?'

'No, no, no – I desire information merely.' He looked at her sharply. 'He attracts you – eh – this young man? *Il est sex appeal?*'

Jane laughed at the phrase.

'No, that's not how I would describe him. He's very simple, but rather a dear.'

'So that is how you describe him – very simple?'

'He *is* simple. I think it's because he's led a nice unworldly life.'

'True,' said Poirot. 'He has not, for instance, dealt with teeth. He has not been disillusioned by the sight of a public hero shivering with fright in the dentist's chair.'

Jane laughed.

'I don't think Norman's roped in any public heroes yet as patients.'

'It would have been a waste, since he is going to Canada.'

'He's talking of New Zealand now. He thinks I'd like the climate better.'

'At all events he is patriotic. He sticks to the British Dominions.'

'I'm hoping,' said Jane, 'that it won't be necessary.'

She fixed Poirot with an inquiring eye.

'Meaning that you put your trust in Papa Poirot? Ah, well – I will do the best I can – that I promise you. But I have the feeling very strongly, Mademoiselle, that there is a figure who has not yet come into the limelight – a part as yet unplayed –'

He shook his head, frowning.

'There is, Mademoiselle, an unknown factor in this case. Everything points to that . . .'

Two days after their arrival in Paris, M. Hercule Poirot and his secretary dined in a small restaurant, and the two Duponts, father and son, were Poirot's guests.

Old M. Dupont, Jane found as charming as his son, but she got little chance of talking to him. Poirot monopolized him severely from the start. Jane found Jean no less easy to get on with than she had done in London. His attractive, boyish personality pleased her now as it had then. He was such a simple friendly soul.

All the same, even while she laughed and talked with him, her ear was alert to catch snatches of the two older men's conversation. She wondered precisely what information it was that Poirot wanted. So far as she could hear, the conversation had never touched once on the murder. Poirot was skilfully drawing out his companion on the subject of the past. His interest in archaeological research in Persia seemed both deep and sincere. M. Dupont was enjoying his evening enormously. Seldom did he get such an intelligent and sympathetic listener.

Whose suggestion it was that the two young people should go to a cinema was not quite clear, but when they had gone Poirot drew his chair a little closer to the table and seemed prepared to take a still more practical interest in archaeological research.

'I comprehend,' he said. 'Naturally it is a great anxiety in these difficult financial days to raise sufficient funds. You accept private donations?'

M. Dupont laughed.

'My dear friend, we sue for them practically on bended knees! But our particular type of dig does not attract the great mass of humanity. They demand spectacular results! Above all, they like gold – large quantities of gold! It is amazing how little the average person cares for pottery. Pottery – the whole romance of humanity can be expressed in terms of pottery. Design – texture –'

M. Dupont was well away. He besought Poirot not to be led astray by the specious publications of B –, the really criminal misdating of L –, and the hopelessly unscientific stratification of G –. Poirot promised solemnly not to be led astray by any of the publications of these learned personages.

Then he said:

'Would a donation, for instance, of five hundred pounds –?'

M. Dupont nearly fell across the table in his excitement.

'You – you are offering that? To me? To aid our researches. But it is magnificent, stupendous! The biggest private donation we have had.'

Poirot coughed.

'I will admit – there is a favour –'

'As, yes, a *souvenir* – some specimens of pottery –'

'No, no, you misunderstand me,' said Poirot quickly before M. Dupont could get well away again. 'It is my secretary – that charming young girl you saw tonight – if she could accompany you on your expedition?'

M. Dupont seemed slightly taken aback for a moment.

'Well,' he said, pulling his moustache, 'it might possibly be arranged. I should have to consult my son. My nephew and his wife are to accompany us. It was to have been a family party. However, I will speak to Jean –'

'Mademoiselle Grey is passionately interested in pottery.

185

The Past has for her an immense fascination. It is the dream of her life to dig. Also she mends socks and sews on buttons in a manner truly admirable.'

'A useful accomplishment.'

'Is it not? And now you were telling me – about the pottery of Susa –'

M. Dupont resumed a happy monologue on his own particular theories of Susa I and Susa II.

Poirot reached his hotel, to find Jane saying good night to Jean Dupont in the hall.

As they went up in the lift Poirot said:

'I have obtained for you a job of great interest. You are to accompany the Duponts to Persia in the spring.'

Jane stared at him.

'Are you quite mad?'

'When the offer is made to you, you will accept with every manifestation of delight.'

'I am certainly not going to Persia. I shall be in Muswell Hill or New Zealand with Norman.'

Poirot twinkled at her gently.

'My dear child,' he said, 'it is some months to next March. To express delight is not to buy a ticket. In the same way, I have talked about a donation – but I have not actually signed a cheque! By the way, I must obtain for you in the morning a handbook on Prehistoric Pottery of the Near East. I have said that you are passionately interested in the subject.'

Jane sighed.

'Being secretary to you is no sinecure, is it? Anything else?'

'Yes. I have said that you sew on buttons and darn socks to perfection.'

'Do I have to give a demonstration of that tomorrow, too?'

'It would be as well, perhaps,' said Poirot, 'if they took my word for it!'

CHAPTER 23

Anne Morisot

At half past ten on the following morning the melancholy M. Fournier walked into Poirot's sitting-room and shook the little Belgian warmly by the hand.

His own manner was far more animated than usual.

'Monsieur,' he said, 'there is something I want to tell you. I have, I think, at last seen the point of what you said in London about the finding of the blowpipe.'

'Ah!' Poirot's face lighted up.

'Yes,' said Fournier taking a chair. 'I pondered much over what you had said. Again and again I say to myself: *Impossible that the crime should have been committed as we believe*. And at last – at last – I see a connexion between that repetition of mine and what you said about the finding of the blowpipe.'

Poirot listened attentively, but said nothing.

'That day in London you said, *Why was the blowpipe found, when it might so easily have been passed out through the ventilator?* And I think now that I have the answer. *The blowpipe was found because the murderer wanted it to be found.*'

'Bravo!' said Poirot.

'That *was* your meaning, then? Good, I thought so. And I went on a step further. I ask myself *Why did the murderer want the blowpipe to be found?* And to that I got the answer: *Because the blowpipe was not used.*'

'Bravo! Bravo! My reasoning exactly.'

'I say to myself: The poisoned dart, *yes*, but not the blowpipe. Then *something else* was used to send that dart through the air – something that a man or woman might put to their lips in a normal manner and which would cause no

187

remark. And I remembered your insistence on a complete list of all that was found in the passengers' luggage and upon their persons. There were two things that especially attracted my attention – *Lady Horbury had two cigarette holders*, and on the table in front of the Duponts *were a number of Kurdish pipes*.'

M. Fournier paused. He looked at Poirot. Poirot did not speak.

'Both those things could have been put to the lips naturally without anyone remarking on it . . . I am right, am I not?'

Poirot hesitated, then he said:

'You are on the right track, yes, but go a little further; and do not forget the wasp.'

'The wasp?' Fournier stared. 'No, there I do not follow you. I cannot see where the wasp comes in.'

'You cannot see? But it is there that I –'

He broke off as the telephone rang.

He took up the receiver.

''Allo, 'allo. Ah, good morning. Yes, it is I myself, Hercule Poirot.' In an aside to Fournier he said, 'It is Thibault . . .'

'Yes – yes, indeed. Very well. And you? M. Fournier? Quite right. Yes, he has arrived. He is here at this moment.'

Lowering the receiver, he said to Fournier:

'He tried to get you at the Sûreté. They told him that you had come to see me here. You had better speak to him. He sounds excited.'

Fournier took the telephone.

''Allo – 'allo. Yes, it is Fournier speaking . . . What . . . *What* . . . In verity, is that so . . .? Yes, indeed . . . Yes . . . Yes, I am sure he will. We will come round at once.'

He replaced the telephone on its hook and looked across at Poirot.

'It is the daughter. The daughter of Madame Giselle.'

'What?'

'Yes, she has arrived to claim her heritage.'

'Where has she come from?'

'America, I understand. Thibault has asked her to return at half past eleven. He suggests we should go round and see him.'

'Most certainly. We will go immediately . . . I will leave a note for Mademoiselle Grey.'

He wrote:

Some developments have occurred which force me to go out. If M. Jean Dupont should ring up or call, be amiable to him. Talk of buttons and socks, but not as yet of prehistoric pottery. He admires you; but he is intelligent!

> *Au revoir,*
> *Hercule Poirot.*

'And now let us come, my friend,' he said, rising. 'This is what I have been waiting for – the entry on the scene of the shadowy figure of whose presence I have been conscious all along. Now – soon – I ought to understand everything.'

Maître Thibault received Poirot and Fournier with great affability.

After an interchange of compliments and polite questions and answers, the lawyer settled down to the discussion of Madame Giselle's heiress.

'I received a letter yesterday,' he said, 'and this morning the young lady herself called upon me.'

'What age is Mademoiselle Morisot?'

'Mademoiselle Morisot – or rather Mrs Richards – for she is married, is exactly twenty-four years of age.'

'She brought documents to prove her identity?' asked Fournier.

'Certainly. Certainly.'

He opened a file at his elbow.

'To begin with, there is this.'

It was a copy of a marriage certificate between George Leman, bachelor, and Marie Morisot – both of Quebec. Its date was 1910. There was also the birth certificate of Anne Morisot Leman. There were various other documents and papers.

'This throws a certain light on the early life of Madame Giselle,' said Fournier.

Thibault nodded.

'As far as I can piece it out,' he said, 'Marie Morisot was nursery governess or sewing-maid when she met this man Leman.

'He was, I gather, a bad lot who deserted her soon after the marriage, and she resumed her maiden name.

'The child was received in the Institut de Marie at Quebec and was brought up there. Marie Morisot or Leman left Quebec shortly afterwards – I imagine with a man – and came to France. She remitted sums of money from time to time, and finally dispatched a lump sum of ready money to be given to the child on attaining the age of twenty-one. At that time Marie Morisot or Leman was, no doubt, living an irregular life, and considered it better to sunder any personal relations.'

'How did the girl realize that she was the heiress to a fortune?'

'We have inserted discreet advertisements in various journals. It seems one of these came to the notice of the Principal of the Institut de Marie, and she wrote or telegraphed to Mrs Richards, who was then in Europe, but on the point of returning to the States.'

'Who is Richards?'

'I gather he is an American or Canadian from Detroit – by profession a maker of surgical instruments.'

'He did not accompany his wife?'

'No, he is still in America.'

'Is Mrs Richards able to throw any light upon a possible reason for her mother's murder?'

The lawyer shook his head.

'She knows nothing about her. In fact, although she had once heard the Principal mention it, she did not even remember what her mother's maiden name was.'

'It looks,' said Fournier, 'as though her appearance on the scene is not going to be of any help in solving the murder problem. Not, I must admit, that I ever thought it would. I am on quite another tack at present. My inquiries have narrowed down to a choice of three persons.'

'Four,' said Poirot.

'You think four?'

'It is not I who say four, but on the theory that you advanced to me you cannot confine yourself to three persons.' He made a sudden rapid motion with his hands. 'The two cigarette holders – the Kurdish pipes and a flute. Remember the flute, my friend.'

Fournier gave an exclamation, but at that moment the door opened and an aged clerk mumbled:

'The lady has returned.'

'Ah,' said Thibault. 'Now you will be able to see the heiress for yourself. Come in, Madame. Let me present to you M. Fournier of the Sûreté, who is in charge in this country of the inquiries into your mother's death. This is M. Hercule Poirot, whose name may be familiar to you and who is kindly giving us his assistance. Madame Richards.'

Giselle's daughter was a dark, chic-looking young woman. She was very smartly though plainly dressed.

She held out her hand to each of the men in turn, murmuring a few appreciative words.

'Though, I fear, Messieurs, that I have hardly the feeling of a daughter in the matter. I have been to all intents and purposes an orphan all my life.'

In answer to Fournier's questions she spoke warmly and gratefully of Mère Angélique, the head of the Institut de Marie.

'She has always been kindness itself to me.'

'You left the Institut – when, Madame?'

'When I was eighteen, Monsieur. I started to earn my

living. I was, for a time, a manicurist. I have also been in a dressmaker's establishment. I met my husband in Nice. He was then just returning to the States. He came over again on business to Holland and we were married in Rotterdam a month ago. Unfortunately, he had to return to Canada. I was detained – but I am now about to rejoin him.'

Anne Richards's French was fluent and easy. She was clearly more French than English.

'You heard of the tragedy – how?'

'Naturally I read of it in the papers, but I did not know – that is, I did not *realize* – that the victim in the case was my mother. Then I received a telegram here in Paris from Mère Angélique giving me the address of Maître Thibault and reminding me of my mother's maiden name.'

Fournier nodded thoughtfully.

They talked a little further, but it seemed clear that Mrs Richards could be of little assistance to them in their search for the murderer. She knew nothing at all of her mother's life or business relations.

Having elicited the name of the hotel at which she was staying, Poirot and Fournier took leave of her.

'You are disappointed, *mon vieux*,' said Fournier. 'You had some idea in your brain about this girl? Did you suspect that she might be an impostor? Or do you, in fact, still suspect that she is an impostor?'

Poirot shook his head in a discouraged manner.

'No – I do not think she is an impostor. Her proofs of identity sound genuine enough . . . It is odd, though, I feel that I have either seen her before – or that she reminds me of someone . . .'

'A likeness to the dead woman?' suggested Fournier doubtfully. 'Surely not.'

'No – it is not that – I wish I could remember what it was. I am sure her face reminds me of someone . . .'

Fournier looked at him curiously.

'You have always, I think, been intrigued by the missing daughter.'

'Naturally,' said Poirot, his eyebrows rising a little. 'Of all the people who may or may not benefit by Giselle's death, this young woman does benefit – very definitely – in hard cash.'

'True – but does that get us anywhere?'

Poirot did not answer for a minute or two. He was following the train of his own thoughts. He said at last:

'My friend – a very large fortune passes to this girl. Do you wonder that from the beginning I speculated as to her being implicated. There were three women on that plane. One of them, Miss Venetia Kerr, was of well-known and authenticated family. But the other two? Ever since Elise Grandier advanced the theory that the father of Madame Giselle's child was an Englishman I have kept it in my mind that one of the two other women might conceivably be this daughter. They were both of approximately the right age. Lady Horbury was a chorus girl whose antecedents were somewhat obscure and who acted under a stage name. Miss Jane Grey, as she once told me, had been brought up in an orphanage.'

'Ah ha!' said the Frenchman. 'So that is the way your mind has been running? Our friend Japp would say that you were being over ingenious.'

'It is true that he always accuses me of preferring to make things difficult.'

'You see?'

'But as a matter of fact it is not true – I proceed always in the simplest manner imaginable! And I never refuse to accept facts.'

'But you are disappointed? You expected more from this Anne Morisot?'

They were just entering Poirot's hotel. An object lying on the reception desk recalled Fournier's mind to something Poirot had said earlier in the morning.

'I have not thanked you,' he said, 'for drawing my attention to the error I had committed. I noted the two cigarette holders of Lady Horbury and the Kurdish pipes of the Duponts. It was unpardonable on my part to have forgotten the flute of Dr Bryant, though I do not seriously suspect him –'

'You do not?'

'No. He does not strike me as the kind of man to –'

He stopped. The man standing at the reception desk talking to the clerk turned, his hand on the flute case. His glance fell on Poirot and his face lit up in grave recognition.

Poirot went forward – Fournier discreetly withdrew into the background. As well that Bryant should not see him.

'Dr Bryant,' said Poirot, bowing.

'M. Poirot.'

They shook hands. A woman who had been standing near Bryant moved away towards the lift. Poirot sent just a fleeting glance after her.

He said:

'Well, *M. le docteur*, are your patients managing to do without you for a little?'

Dr Bryant smiled – that melancholy attractive smile that the other remembered so well. He looked tired, but strangely peaceful.

'I have no patients now,' he said.

Then, moving towards a little table, he said:

'A glass of sherry, M. Poirot, or some other *apéritif?*'

'I thank you.'

They sat down, and the doctor gave the order. Then he said slowly:

'No, I have no patients now. I have retired.'

'A sudden decision?'

'Not so very sudden.'

He was silent as the drinks were set before them. Then, raising the glass, he said:

'It is a necessary decision. I resign of my own free will before I am struck off the register.' He went on speaking in a gentle, far-away voice. 'There comes to everyone a turning-point in their lives, M. Poirot. They stand at the cross-roads and have to decide. My profession interests me enormously – it is a sorrow – a very great sorrow to abandon it. But there are other claims . . . There is, M. Poirot, the happiness of a human being.'

Poirot did not speak. He waited.

'There is a lady – a patient of mine – I love her very dearly. She has a husband who causes her infinite misery. He takes drugs. If you were a doctor you would know what that meant. She has no money of her own, so she cannot leave him . . .

'For some time I have been undecided – but now I have made up my mind. She and I are now on our way to Kenya to begin a new life. I hope that at last she may know a little happiness. She has suffered so long . . .'

Again he was silent. Then he said in a brisker tone:

'I tell you this, M. Poirot, because it will soon be public property, and the sooner you know the better.'

'I understand,' said Poirot. After a minute he said, 'You take your flute, I see?'

Dr Bryant smiled.

'My flute, M. Poirot, is my oldest companion . . . When everything else fails – music remains.'

His hand ran lovingly over the flute case, then with a bow he rose.

Poirot rose also.

'My best wishes for your future, *M. le docteur* – and for that of Madame,' said Poirot.

When Fournier rejoined his friend, Poirot was at the desk making arrangements for a trunk call to Quebec.

CHAPTER 24

A Broken Finger-Nail

'What now?' cried Fournier. 'You are still preoccupied with this girl who inherits? Decidedly it is the *idée fixe* you have there.'

'Not at all, not at all,' said Poirot. 'But there must be in all things order and method. One must finish with one thing before proceeding to the next.'

He looked round.

'Here is Mademoiselle Jane. Suppose that you commence *déjeuner*. I will join you as soon as I can.'

Fournier acquiesced and he and Jane went into the dining-room.

'Well?' said Jane with curiosity. 'What is she like?'

'She is a little over medium height, dark, with a matte complexion, a pointed chin –'

'You're talking exactly like a passport,' said Jane. 'My passport description is simply insulting, I think. It's composed of mediums and ordinary. Nose, medium; mouth ordinary (how do they expect you to describe a mouth?); forehead, ordinary; chin, ordinary.'

'But not ordinary eyes,' said Fournier.

'Even they are grey, which is not a very exciting colour.'

'And who has told you, Mademoiselle, that it is not an exciting colour?' said the Frenchman, leaning across the table.

Jane laughed.

'Your command of the English language,' she said, 'is highly efficient. Tell me more about Anne Morisot – is she pretty?'

'*Assez bien*,' said Fournier cautiously. 'And she is not Anne Morisot. She is Anne Richards. She is married.'

'Was the husband there, too?'

'No.'

'Why not, I wonder?'

'Because he is in Canada or America.'

He explained some of the circumstances of Anne's life. Just as he was drawing his narrative to a close, Poirot joined them.

He looked a little dejected.

'Well, *mon cher*?' inquired Fournier.

'I spoke to the principal – to Mère Angélique herself. It is romantic, you know, the transatlantic telephone. To speak so easily to someone nearly halfway across the globe.'

'The telegraphed photograph – that too is romantic. Science is the greatest romance there is. But you were saying?'

'I talked with Mère Angélique. She confirmed exactly what Mrs Richards told us of the circumstances of her having been brought up at the Institut de Marie. She spoke quite frankly about the mother who left Quebec with a Frenchman interested in the wine trade. She was relieved at the time that the child would not come under her mother's influence. From her point of view Giselle was on the downward path. Money was sent regularly – but Giselle never suggested a meeting.'

'In fact your conversation was a repetition of what we heard this morning.'

'Practically – except that it was more detailed. Anne Morisot left the Institut de Marie six years ago to become a manicurist, afterwards she had a job as a lady's maid – and finally left Quebec for Europe in that capacity. Her letters were not frequent, but Mère Angélique usually heard from her about twice a year. When she saw an account of the inquest in the paper she realized that this Marie Morisot was in all probability the Marie Morisot who had lived in Quebec.'

'What about the husband?' asked Fournier. 'Now that we know definitely that Giselle was married, the husband might become a factor?'

'I thought of that. It was one of the reasons for my telephone call. George Leman, Giselle's blackguard of a husband, was killed in the early days of the war.'

He paused and then remarked abruptly:

'What was it that I just said – not my last remark – the one before? – I have an idea that – without knowing it – I said something of significance.'

Fournier repeated as well as he could the substance of Poirot's remarks, but the little man shook his head in a dissatisfied manner.

'No – no – it was not that. Well, no matter . . .'

He turned to Jane and engaged her in conversation.

At the close of the meal he suggested that they have coffee in the lounge.

Jane agreed and stretched out her hand for her bag and gloves, which were on the table. As she picked them up she winced slightly.

'What is it, Mademoiselle?'

'Oh, it's nothing,' laughed Jane. 'It's only a jagged nail. I must file it.'

Poirot sat down again very suddenly.

'*Nom d'un nom d'un nom*,' he said quietly.

The other two stared at him in surprise.

'M. Poirot?' cried Jane. 'What is it?'

'It is,' said Poirot, 'that I remember now why the face of Anne Morisot is familiar to me. I have seen her before . . . in the aeroplane on the day of the murder. Lady Horbury sent for her to get a nail file. *Anne Morisot was Lady Horbury's maid.*'

CHAPTER 25

'I Am Afraid'

This sudden revelation had an almost stunning effect on the three people sitting round the luncheon table. It opened up an entirely new aspect of the case.

Instead of being a person wholly remote from the tragedy, Anne Morisot was now shown to have been actually present on the scene of the crime. It took a minute or two for everyone to readjust their ideas.

Poirot made a frantic gesture with his hands – his eyes closed – his face contorted in agony.

'A little minute – a little minute,' he implored them. 'I have got to think, to see, to realize how this affects my ideas of the case. I must go back in my mind. I must remember . . . A thousand maledictions on my unfortunate stomach. I was preoccupied only with my internal sensations!'

'She was actually on the plane, then,' said Fournier. 'I see. I begin to see.'

'I remember,' said Jane. 'A tall, dark girl.' Her eyes half closed in an effort of memory. 'Madeleine, Lady Horbury called her.'

'That is it, Madeleine,' said Poirot.

'Lady Horbury sent her along to the end of the plane to fetch a case – a scarlet dressing-case.'

'You mean,' said Fournier, 'that this girl went right past the seat where her mother was sitting?'

'That is right.'

'The motive,' said Fournier. He gave a great sigh. 'And the opportunity . . . Yes, it is all there.'

Then with a sudden vehemence most unlike his usual melancholy manner, he brought down his hand with a bang on the table.

'But, *parbleu*!' he cried. 'Why did no one mention this before? Why was she not included amongst the suspected persons?'

'I have told you, my friend. I have told you,' said Poirot wearily. 'My unfortunate stomach.'

'Yes, yes, that is understandable. But there were other stomachs unaffected – the stewards', the other passengers'.'

'I think,' said Jane, 'that perhaps it was because it was so very early this happened. The plane had only just left Le Bourget; and Giselle was alive and well an hour or so after that. It seemed as though she must have been killed much later.'

'That is curious,' said Fournier thoughtfully. 'Can there have been a delayed action of the poison? Such things happen . . .'

Poirot groaned and dropped his head into his hands.

'I must think. I must think . . . Can it be possible that all along my ideas have been entirely wrong?'

'*Mon vieux*,' said Fournier, 'such things happen. They happen to me. It is possible that they have happened to you. One has occasionally to pocket one's pride and readjust one's ideas.'

'That is true,' agreed Poirot. 'It is possible that all along I have attached too much importance to one particular thing. I expected to find a certain clue. I found it, and I built up my case from it. But if I have been wrong from the beginning – if that particular article was where it was merely as the result of an *accident* . . . why, then – yes – I will admit that I have been wrong – completely wrong.'

'You cannot shut your eyes to the importance of this turn of events,' said Fournier. 'Motive and opportunity – what more can you want?'

'Nothing. It must be as you say. The delayed action of the poison is indeed extraordinary – practically speaking – one would say *impossible*. But where poisons are concerned the impossible does happen. One has to reckon with idiosyncrasy . . .'

His voice tailed off.

'We must discuss a plan of campaign,' said Fournier. 'For the moment it would, I think, be unwise to arouse Anne Morisot's suspicions. She is completely unaware that you have recognized her. Her *bona fides* has been accepted. We know the hotel at which she is staying and we can keep in touch with her through Thibault. Legal formalities can always be delayed. We have two points established – opportunity and motive. We have still to prove that Anne Morisot had snake venom in her possession. There is also the question of the American who bought the blowpipe and bribed Jules Perrot. It might certainly be the husband – Richards. We have only her word for it that he is in Canada.'

'As you say – the husband . . . Yes, the husband. Ah, wait – wait!'

Poirot pressed his hands upon his temples.

'It is all wrong,' he murmured. 'I do not employ the little grey cells of the brain in an orderly and methodical way. No, I leap to conclusions. I think, perhaps, what I am *meant* to think. No, that is wrong again. If my original idea were right, I could not be *meant* to think –'

He broke off.

'I beg your pardon,' said Jane.

Poirot did not answer for a moment or two; then he took his hands from his temples, sat very upright and straightened two forks and a salt-cellar which offended his sense of symmetry.

'Let us reason,' he said. 'Anne Morisot is either guilty or innocent of the crime. If she is innocent why has she lied? Why has she concealed the fact that she was lady's maid to Lady Horbury?'

'Why, indeed?' said Fournier.

'So we say Anne Morisot is guilty because she has lied. But wait. Suppose my first supposition was correct. Will that supposition fit in with Anne Morisot's guilt, or with Anne Morisot's lie? Yes – yes – it *might* – given one premise. But in that case – and if that premise is correct – *then Anne Morisot should not have been on the plane at all.*'

The others looked at him politely, if with, perhaps, a rather perfunctory interest.

Fournier thought:

'I see now what the Englishman, Japp, meant. He makes difficulties, this old one. He tries to make an affair which is now simple sound complicated. He cannot accept a straightforward solution without pretending that it squares with his preconceived ideas.'

Jane thought:

'I don't see in the least what he means . . . Why couldn't the girl be in the plane? She had to go wherever Lady Horbury wanted her to go . . . I think he's rather a mountebank, really . . .'

Suddenly Poirot drew in his breath with a hiss.

'Of course,' he said. 'It is a possibility; and it ought to be very simple to find out.'

He rose.

'What now, my friend?' asked Fournier.

'Again the telephone,' said Poirot.

'The transatlantic to Quebec?'

'This time it is merely a call to London.'

'To Scotland Yard?'

'No, to Lord Horbury's house in Grosvenor Square. If only I have the good fortune to find Lady Horbury at home.'

'Be careful, my friend. If any suspicion gets round to Anne Morisot that we have been making inquiries about her it would not suit our affairs. Above all, we must not put her upon her guard.'

'Have no fears. I will be discreet. I ask only one little question – a question of a most harmless nature.' He smiled. 'You shall come with me if you like.'

'No, no.'

'But yes. I insist.'

The two men went off, leaving Jane in the lounge.

It took some little time to put the call through; but Poirot's luck was in. Lady Horbury was lunching at home.

'Good. Will you tell Lady Horbury that it is M. Hercule Poirot speaking from Paris.' There was a pause. 'That is you, Lady Horbury? No, no, all is well. I assure you *all is well*. It is not that matter at all. I want you to answer me a question. Yes . . . When you go from Paris to England by air does your maid usually go with you, or does she go by train? By train . . . And so on that particular occasion . . . I see . . . You are sure? Ah, she has left you. I see. She left you very suddenly at a moment's notice. *Mais oui*, base ingratitude. It is too true. A most ungrateful class! Yes, yes, exactly. No, no, you need not worry. *Au revoir*. Thank you.'

He replaced the receiver and turned to Fournier, his eyes green and shining.

'Listen, my friend, *Lady Horbury's maid usually travelled by train and boat*. On the occasion of Giselle's murder Lady Horbury decided *at the last moment* that Madeleine had better go by air, too.'

He took the Frenchman by the arm.

'Quick, my friend,' he said. 'We must go to her hotel. If my little idea is correct – and I think it is – there is no time to be lost.'

Fournier stared at him. But before he could frame a question Poirot had turned away and was heading for the revolving doors leading out of the hotel.

Fournier hastened after him.

'But I do not understand. What is all this?'

The commissionaire was holding open the door of a taxi. Poirot jumped in and gave the address of Anne Morisot's hotel.

'And drive quickly, but quickly!'

Fournier jumped in after him.

'What fly is this that has bitten you? Why this mad rush – this haste?'

'Because, my friend, if, as I say, my little idea is correct – *Anne Morisot is in imminent danger*.'

'You think so?'

Fournier could not help a sceptical tone creeping into his voice.

'I am afraid,' said Poirot. 'Afraid. *Bon Dieu* – how this taxi crawls!'

The taxi at the moment was doing a good forty miles an hour and cutting in and out of traffic with a miraculous immunity due to the excellent eye of the driver.

'It crawls to such an extent that we shall have an accident in a minute,' said Fournier drily. 'And Mademoiselle Grey, we have left her planted there awaiting our return from the telephone, and instead we leave the hotel without a word. It is not very polite, that!'

'Politeness or impoliteness – what does it matter in an affair of life and death?'

'Life or death?' Fournier shrugged his shoulders.

He thought to himself:

'It is all very well, but this obstinate madman may endanger the whole business. Once the girl knows that we are on her track –'

He said in a persuasive voice:

'See now, M. Poirot, be reasonable. We must go carefully.'

'You do not understand,' said Poirot. 'I am afraid – afraid –'

The taxi drew up with a jerk at the quiet hotel where Anne Morisot was staying.

Poirot sprang out and nearly collided with a young man just leaving the hotel.

Poirot stopped dead for a moment, looking after him.

'Another face that I know – but where –? Ah, I remember – it is the actor Raymond Barraclough.'

As he stepped forward to enter the hotel, Fournier placed a restraining hand on his arm.

'M. Poirot, I have the utmost respect, the utmost admiration for your methods – but I feel very strongly that no precipitate action must be taken. I am responsible here in France for the conduct of this case . . .'

Poirot interrupted him:

'I comprehend your anxiety; but do not fear any "precipitate action" on my part. Let us make inquiries at the desk. If Madame Richards is here and all is well – then no harm is done – and we can discuss together our future action. You do not object to that?'

'No, no, of course not.'

'Good.'

Poirot passed through the revolving door and went up to the reception desk. Fournier followed him.

'You have a Mrs Richards staying here, I believe,' said Poirot.

'No, Monsieur. She was staying here, but she left today.'

'She has left?' demanded Fournier.

'Yes, Monsieur.'

'When did she leave?'

The clerk glanced up at the clock.

'A little over half an hour ago.'

'Was her departure unexpected? Where has she gone?'

The clerk stiffened at the questions and was disposed to refuse to answer; but when Fournier's credentials were produced the clerk changed his tone and was eager to give any assistance in his power.

No, the lady had not left an address. He thought her departure was the result of a sudden change of plans. She had formerly said she was making a stay of about a week.

More questions. The concierge was summoned, the luggage porters, the lift boys.

According to the concierge a gentleman had called to see the lady. He had come while she was out, but had awaited her return, and they had lunched together. What kind of gentleman? An American gentleman – very American. She had seemed surprised to see him. After lunch the lady gave orders for her luggage to be brought down and put on a taxi.

Where had she driven to? She had driven to the Gare du Nord – at least that is the order she had given to the taximan. Did the American gentleman go with her? No, she had gone alone.

'The Gare du Nord,' said Fournier. 'That means England on the face of it. The two o'clock service. But it may be a blind. We must telephone to Boulogne and also try and get hold of that taxi.'

It was as though Poirot's fears had communicated themselves to Fournier.

The Frenchman's face was anxious.

Rapidly and efficiently he set the machinery of the law in motion.

It was five o'clock when Jane, sitting in the lounge of the hotel with a book, looked up to see Poirot coming towards her.

She opened her mouth reproachfully, but the words remained unspoken. Something in his face stopped her.

'What was it?' she said. 'Has anything happened?'

Poirot took both her hands in his.

'Life is very terrible, Mademoiselle,' he said.

Something in his tone made Jane feel frightened.

'What is it?' she said again.

Poirot said slowly:

'When the boat train reached Boulogne they found a woman in a first-class carriage – dead.'

The colour ebbed from Jane's face.

'Anne Morisot?'

'Anne Morisot. In her hand was a little blue glass bottle which had contained hydrocyanic acid.'

'Oh!' said Jane. 'Suicide?'

Poirot did not answer for a moment or two. Then he said, with the air of one who chooses his words carefully:

'Yes, the police think it was suicide.'

'And you?'

Poirot slowly spread out his hands in an expressive gesture.

'What else – is there to think?'

'She killed herself – why? Because of remorse – or because she was afraid of being found out?'

Poirot shook his head.

'Life can be very terrible,' he said. 'One needs much courage.'

'To kill oneself? Yes, I suppose one does.'

'Also to live,' said Poirot, 'one needs courage.'

CHAPTER 26

After Dinner Speech

The next day Poirot left Paris. Jane stayed behind with a list of duties to perform. Most of these seemed singularly meaningless to her, but she carried them out to the best of her powers. She saw Jean Dupont twice. He mentioned the expedition which she was to join, and Jane did not dare to undeceive him without orders from Poirot, so she hedged as best she could and turned the conversation to other matters.

Five days later she was recalled to England by a telegram.

Norman met her at Victoria and they discussed recent events.

Very little publicity had been given to the suicide. There had been a paragraph in the papers stating that a Canadian lady, a Mrs Richards, had committed suicide in the Paris-Boulogne express, but that was all. There had been no mention of any connexion with the aeroplane murder.

Both Norman and Jane were inclined to be jubilant. Their troubles, they hoped, were at an end. Norman was not so sanguine as Jane.

'They may suspect of her of doing her mother in, but now that she's taken this way out they probably won't bother to go on with the case; and unless it is proved publicly I don't see what good it is going to be to all of us poor devils. From the point of view of the public we shall remain under suspicion just as much as ever!'

He said as much to Poirot, whom he met a few days later in Piccadilly.

Poirot smiled.

'You are like all the rest. You think I am an old man

who accomplishes nothing! Listen, you shall come tonight to dine with me. Japp is coming, and also our friend Mr Clancy. I have some things to say that may be interesting.'

The dinner passed off pleasantly. Japp was patronizing and good humoured, Norman was interested, and little Mr Clancy was nearly as thrilled as when he had recognized the fatal thorn.

It seemed clear that Poirot was not above trying to impress the little author.

After dinner, when coffee had been drunk, Poirot cleared his throat in a slightly embarrassed manner, not free from self-importance.

'My friends,' he said, 'Mr Clancy here has expressed interest in what he would call "my methods, Watson". (*C'est ça, n'est-ce pas?*) I propose, if it will not bore you all' – he paused significantly, and Norman and Japp said quickly, 'No, no,' and 'Most interesting' – 'to give you a little résumé of my methods in dealing with this case.'

He paused and consulted some notes. Japp whispered to Norman:

'Fancies himself, doesn't he? Conceit's that little man's middle name.'

Poirot looked at him reproachfully and said, 'Ahem!'

Three politely interested faces were turned to him, and he began:

'I will start at the beginning, my friends. I will go back to the air liner *Prometheus* on its ill-fated journey from Paris to Croydon. I am going to tell you my precise ideas and impressions at the time – passing on to how I came to confirm or modify them in the light of future events.

'When, just before we reached Croydon, Dr Bryant was approached by the steward and went with him to examine the body, I accompanied him. I had a feeling that it might – who knows? – be something in my line. I have, perhaps, too professional a point of view where deaths are concerned. They are divided, in my mind, into two classes – deaths which are my affair and deaths which are not my affair – and though the latter class is infinitely more numerous – nevertheless whenever I come in contact with death I am like the dog who lifts his head and sniffs the scent.

'Dr Bryant confirmed the steward's fear that the woman was dead. As to the cause of death, naturally he could not pronounce on that without a detailed examination. It was at this point that a suggestion was made – by M. Jean Dupont – that death was due to shock following on a wasp sting. In furtherance of this hypothesis, he drew attention to a wasp that he himself had slaughtered shortly before.

'Now that was a perfectly plausible theory – and one quite likely to be accepted. There was the mark on the dead woman's neck – closely resembling the mark of a sting – and there was the fact that a wasp had been in the plane.

'But at that moment I was fortunate enough to look down and espy what might at first have been taken for the body of yet another wasp. In actuality it was a native thorn with a little teased yellow and black silk on it.

'At this point Mr Clancy came forward and made the statement that it was a thorn shot from a blowpipe after the manner of some native tribe. Later, as you all know, the blowpipe itself was discovered.

'By the time we reached Croydon several ideas were working in my mind. Once I was definitely on the firm ground, my brain began to work once more with its normal brilliance.'

'Go it, M. Poirot,' said Japp with a grin. 'Don't have any false modesty.'

Poirot threw him a look and went on.

'One idea presented itself very strongly to me (as it did to everyone else), and that was the audacity of a crime being committed in such a manner – and the astonishing fact that nobody noticed its being done!

'There were two other points that interested me. One was the convenient presence of the wasp. The other was the discovery of the blowpipe. As I remarked after the inquest to my friend Japp, why on earth did the murderer not get rid of it by passing it out through the ventilating hole in the window? The thorn itself might be difficult to trace or identify, but a blowpipe which still retained a portion of its price label was a very different matter.

'What was the solution? Obviously that the murderer *wanted* the blowpipe to be found.

'But why? Only one answer seemed logical. If a poisoned dart and a blowpipe were found, it would naturally be assumed that the murder had been committed by a thorn shot from a blowpipe. Therefore in reality the murder had *not* been committed that way.

'On the other hand, as medical evidence was to show, the cause of death *was* undoubtedly the poisoned thorn. I shut my eyes and asked myself – what is the surest and most reliable way of placing a poisoned thorn in the jugular vein? And the answer came immediately: *By hand*.

'And that immediately threw light on the necessity for the finding of the blowpipe. The blowpipe inevitably conveyed the suggestion of *distance*. If my theory was right, the person who killed Madame Giselle was a person who went right up to her table and bent over her.

'Was there such a person? Yes, there were two people. The two stewards. Either of them could go up to Madame Giselle, lean towards her, and nobody would notice anything unusual.

'Was there anyone else?

'Well, there was Mr Clancy. He was the only person in the car who had passed immediately by Madame Giselle's seat – and I remembered that it was he who had first drawn attention to the blowpipe and thorn theory.'

Mr Clancy sprang to his feet.

'I protest,' he cried. 'I protest. This is an outrage.'

'Sit down,' said Poirot. 'I have not finished yet. I have to show you all the steps by which I arrived at my conclusion.

211

'I had now three persons as possible suspects – Mitchell, Davis, and Mr Clancy. None of them at first sight appeared likely murderers, but there was much investigation to be done.

'I next turned my mind to the possibilities of the wasp. It was suggestive, that wasp. To begin with, no one had noticed it until about the time coffee was served. That in itself was rather curious. I constructed a certain theory of the crime. The murderer presented to the world two separate solutions of the tragedy. On the first or simplest, Madame Giselle was stung by a wasp and had succumbed to heart failure. The success of that solution depended on whether or no the murderer was in a position to retrieve the thorn. Japp and I agreed that that could be done easily enough – *so long as no suspicion of foul play had arisen.* There was the particular colouring of silk which I had no doubt was deliberately substituted for the original cerise so as to simulate the appearance of a wasp.

'Our murderer, then, approaches the victim's table, inserts the thorn and releases the wasp! The poison is so powerful that death would occur almost immediately. If Giselle cried out – it would probably not be heard owing to the noise of the plane. If it was just noticed, well, there was the wasp buzzing about to explain the cry. The poor woman had been stung.

'That, as I say, was plan No. 1. *But supposing that, as actually happened, the poisoned thorn was discovered* before the murderer could retrieve it. In that case the fat is in the fire. The theory of natural death is impossible. Instead of getting rid of the blowpipe through the window, it is put in a place where it is bound to be discovered when the plane is searched; and at once it will be assumed that the blowpipe was the instrument of the crime. The proper atmosphere of distance will be created and when the blowpipe is traced it will focus suspicion in a definite and prearranged direction.

'I had now my theory of the crime, and I had three

suspects with a barely possible fourth – M. Jean Dupont, who had outlined the "Death by a Wasp Sting theory", and who was sitting on the gangway so near Giselle that he might just possibly have moved from it without being noticed. On the other hand, I did not really think he would have dared to take such a risk.

'I concentrated on the problem of the wasp. If the murderer had brought the wasp on to the plane and released it at the psychological moment – he must have had something in the nature of a small box in which to keep it.

'Hence my interest in the contents of the passengers' pockets and hand luggage.

'And here I came up against a totally unexpected development. I found what I was looking for – but as it seemed to me on the wrong person. There was an empty small-sized Bryant & May's match-box in Mr Norman Gale's pocket. *But by everybody's evidence Mr Gale had never passed down the gangway of the car*. He had only visited the toilet compartment and returned to his own seat.

'Nevertheless, although it seems *impossible*, there *was* a method by which Mr Gale could have committed the crime – as the contents of his attaché-case showed.'

'My attaché-case?' said Norman Gale. He looked amused and puzzled. 'Why, I don't even remember now what was in it.'

Poirot smiled at him amiably.

'Wait a little minute. I will come to that. I am telling you my first ideas.

'To proceed – I had *four* persons who could have done the crime – from the point of view of *possibility*: the two stewards, Clancy and Gale.

'I now looked at the case from the *opposite* angle – that of motive – if a *motive* were to coincide with a *possibility* – well, I had my murderer! But alas, I could find nothing of the kind. My friend Japp has accused me of liking to make things difficult. On the contrary, I approached this question of motive with all the simplicity in the world. To whose benefit would it be if Madame Giselle were removed? Clearly to her unknown daughter's benefit – since that unknown daughter would inherit a fortune. There were also certain persons who were in Madame Giselle's power, or shall we say – who *might* be in Giselle's power, for aught we knew. That, then, was a task of elimination. Of the passengers in the plane I could only be certain of one who was undoubtedly mixed up with Giselle. That one was Lady Horbury.

'In Lady Horbury's case the motive was very clear. She had visited Giselle at her house in Paris the night before. She was desperate and she had a friend, a young actor, who might easily have impersonated the American who bought the blowpipe – and might also have bribed the clerk in Universal Airlines to ensure that Giselle travelled by the 12 o'clock service.

'I had, as it were, a problem in two halves. I did not see how it was *possible* for Lady Horbury to commit the crime; and I could not see for what *motive* the stewards, Mr Clancy, or Mr Gale should want to commit it.

'Always, in the back of my mind, I considered the problem of Giselle's unknown daughter and heiress. Were any of my four suspects married – and if so, could one of the wives be this Anne Morisot? If her father was English, the girl might have been brought up in England. Mitchell's wife I soon dismissed – she was of good old Dorset stock. Davis was courting a girl whose father and mother were alive. Mr Clancy was not married. Mr Gale was obviously head over ears in love with Miss Jane Grey.

'I may say that I investigated the antecedents of Miss Grey very carefully, having learned from her in casual conversation that she had been brought up in an orphanage near Dublin. But I soon satisfied myself that Miss Grey was *not* Madame Giselle's daughter.

'I made out a table of results – the stewards had neither gained nor lost by Madame Giselle's death – except that Mitchell was obviously suffering from shock. Mr Clancy was planning a book on the subject by which he hoped to make money. Mr Gale was fast losing his practice. Nothing very helpful there.

'And yet, at that time, *I was convinced that Mr Gale was the murderer* – there was the empty match-box – the contents of his attaché-case. Apparently he *lost*, not gained, by the death of Giselle. But those appearances might be *false* appearances.

'I determined to cultivate his acquaintance. It is my experience that no one, in the course of conversation, can fail to give themselves away sooner or later . . . Everyone has an irresistible urge to talk about themselves.

'I tried to gain Mr Gale's confidence. I pretended to confide in him, and I even enlisted his help. I persuaded him to aid me in the fake blackmailing of Lady Horbury. And it was then that he made his first mistake.

'I had suggested a slight disguise. He arrived to play his part with a ridiculous and impossible outfit! The whole thing was a farce. No one, I felt sure, could play a part as *badly* as he was proposing to play one. What then was the reason for this? *Because his knowledge of his own guilt* made him chary of showing himself to be a good actor. When, however, I had adjusted his ridiculous makeup, his artistic skill showed itself. He played his part perfectly and Lady Horbury did not recognize him. I was convinced then that he could have disguised himself as an American in Paris and could also have played the necessary part in the *Prometheus*.

'By this time I was getting seriously worried about Mademoiselle Jane. Either she was in this business with him, or else she was entirely innocent – and in the latter case she was a victim. She might wake up one day to find herself married to a murderer.

With the object of preventing a precipitate marriage, I took Mademoiselle Jane to Paris as my secretary.

'It was whilst we were there that the missing heiress appeared to claim her fortune. I was haunted by a resemblance that I could not place. I did place it in the end – but too late . . .

'At first the discovery that she had actually been in the plane *and had lied about it* seemed to overthrow all my theories. Here, overwhelmingly, was the guilty person.

'But if she were guilty she had an accomplice – the man who bought the blowpipe and bribed Jules Perrot.

'Who was that man? Was it conceivably her husband?

'And – then – suddenly I saw the true solution. True, that is, if one point could be verified.

'For my solution to be correct Anne Morisot ought not to have been on the plane.

'I rang up Lady Horbury and got my answer. The maid, Madeleine, travelled in the plane by a last-minute whim of her mistress.'

He stopped.

Mr Clancy said:

'Ahem – but – I'm afraid I'm not quite clear.'

'When did you stop pitching on me as the murderer?' asked Norman.

Poirot wheeled round on him.

'I never stopped. *You are the murderer* . . . Wait – I will tell you everything. For the last week Japp and I have been busy – It is true that you became a dentist to please your uncle – John Gale. You took his name when you came into partnership with him – but you were his *sister's* son – not his brother's. Your real name is *Richards*. It was as Richards that you met the girl Anne Morisot at Nice last winter, when she was there with her mistress. The story she told us was true as to the facts of her childhood, but the latter part was edited carefully by you. She *did* know her mother's maiden name. Giselle was at Monte Carlo – she was pointed out and her real name was mentioned. You realized that there might be a large fortune to be got. It appealed to your gambler's nature. It was from Anne Morisot that you learnt of Lady Horbury's connexion with Giselle. The plan of the crime formed itself in your head. Giselle was to be murdered in such a way that suspicion would fall on Lady

Horbury. Your plans matured and finally fructified. You bribed the clerk in Universal Airlines so that Giselle should travel on the same plane as Lady Horbury. Anne Morisot had told you that she herself was going to England by train – you never expected her to be on the plane – and it seriously jeopardized your plans. If it was once known that Giselle's daughter and heiress had been on the plane suspicion would naturally have fallen upon her. Your original idea was that she should claim the inheritance with a perfect alibi, since she would have been on a train or boat at the time of the crime; and then you would have married her.

'The girl was by this time infatuated with you. But it was money you were after – not the girl herself.

'There was another complication to your plans. At Le Pinet you saw Mademoiselle Jane Grey and fell madly in love with her. Your passion for her drove you on to play a much more dangerous game.

'You intended to have both the money and the girl you loved. You were committing a murder for the sake of money, and you were in no mind to relinquish the fruits of the crime. You frightened Anne Morisot by telling her that if she came forward at once to proclaim her identity she would certainly be suspected of the murder. Instead you induced her to ask for a few days' leave, and you went together to Rotterdam, where you were married.

'In due course you primed her how to claim the money. She was to say nothing of her employment as lady's maid, and it was very clearly to be made plain that she and her husband had been abroad at the time of the murder.

'Unfortunately, the date planned for Anne Morisot to go to Paris and claim her inheritance coincided with my arrival in Paris, where Miss Grey had accompanied me. That did not suit your book at all. Either Mademoiselle Jane or myself *might* recognize in Anne Morisot the Madeleine who had been Lady Horbury's maid.

'You tried to get in touch with her in time, but failed.

You finally arrived in Paris yourself and found she had already gone to the lawyer. When she returned she told you of her meeting with me. Things were becoming dangerous, and you made up your mind to act quickly.

'It had been your intention that your new-made wife should not survive her accession to wealth very long. Immediately after the marriage ceremony you had both made wills leaving all you had one to the other! A very touching business.

'You intended, I fancy, to follow a fairly leisurely course. You would have gone to Canada – ostensibly because of the failure of your practice. There you would have resumed the name of Richards and your wife would have rejoined you. All the same I do not fancy it would have been very long before Mrs Richards regrettably died, leaving a fortune to a seemingly inconsolable widower. You would then have returned to England as Norman Gale, having had the good fortune to make a lucky speculation in Canada! But now you decided that no time must be lost.'

Poirot paused and Norman Gale threw back his head and laughed.

'You are very clever at knowing what people intend to do! You ought to adopt Mr Clancy's profession!' His tone deepened to one of anger. 'I never heard such a farrago of nonsense. What you *imagined*, M. Poirot, is hardly evidence!'

Poirot did not seem put out. He said:

'Perhaps not. But, then, I *have* some evidence.'

'Really?' sneered Norman. 'Perhaps you have *evidence* as to how I killed old Giselle when everyone in the aeroplane knows perfectly well I never went near her?'

'I will tell you *exactly how you committed the crime*,' said Poirot. '*What about the contents of your dispatch-case?* You were on a holiday. *Why take a dentist's linen coat*? That is what I asked myself. And the answer is this – because it resembled so closely a *steward's coat* . . .

218

'That is what you did. When coffee was served and the stewards had gone to the other compartment you went to the toilet, put on your linen coat, padded your cheeks with cottonwool rolls, came out, seized a coffee spoon from the box in the pantry opposite, hurried down the gangway with the steward's quick run, spoon in hand, to Giselle's table. You thrust the thorn into her neck, opened the match-box and let the wasp escape, hurried back into the toilet, changed your coat and emerged leisurely to return to your table. The whole thing took only a couple of minutes.

'*Nobody notices a steward particularly*. The only person who might have recognized you was Mademoiselle Jane. But you know women! As soon as a woman is left alone (particularly when she is travelling with an attractive young man) she seizes the opportunity to have a good look in her hand mirror, powder her nose and adjust her makeup.'

'Really,' sneered Gale. 'A most interesting theory; but it didn't happen. Anything else?'

'Quite a lot,' said Poirot. 'As I have just said, in the course of conversation a man gives himself away . . . You were imprudent enough to mention that for a while you were *on a farm in South Africa*. What you did not say, but what I have since found out, is that it was a *snake farm* . . .'

For the first time Norman Gale showed fear. He tried to speak, but the words would not come.

Poirot continued:

'You were there under your own name of Richards; *a photograph of you transmitted by telephone has been recognized*. That same photograph has been identified in Rotterdam as the man Richards who married Anne Morisot.'

Again Norman Gale tried to speak and failed. His whole personality seemed to change. The handsome, vigorous young man turned into a rat-like creature with furtive eyes looking for a way of escape and finding none . . .

'It was haste ruined your plan,' said Poirot. 'The Superior of the Institut de Marie hurried things on by wiring to Anne

Morisot. It would have looked suspicious to ignore that wire. You had impressed it upon your wife that unless she suppressed certain facts either she or you might be suspected of murder, since you had both unfortunately been in the plane when Giselle was killed. When you met her afterwards and you learnt that I had been present at the interview you hurried things on. You were afraid I might get the truth out of Anne – perhaps she herself was beginning to suspect you. You hustled her away out of the hotel and into the boat train. You administered prussic acid to her by force and you left the empty bottle in her hand.'

'A lot of damned lies . . .'

'Oh, no. There was a bruise on her neck.'

'Damned lies, I tell you.'

'You even left your fingerprints on the bottle.'

'You lie. I wore –'

'Ah, you wore gloves . . . ? I think, Monsieur, that little admission cooks your gander.'

'You damned interfering little mountebank!' Livid with passion, his face unrecognizable, Gale made a spring at Poirot. Japp, however, was too quick for him. Holding him in a capable unemotional grip, Japp said:

'James Richards, alias Norman Gale, I hold a warrant for your arrest on the charge of wilful murder. I must warn you that anything you say will be taken down and used in evidence.'

A terrible shudder shook the man. He seemed on the point of collapse.

A couple of plain-clothes men were waiting outside. Norman Gale was taken away.

Left alone with Poirot, little Mr Clancy drew a deep breath of ecstasy.

'M. Poirot,' he said. 'That has been absolutely the most thrilling experience of my life. You have been wonderful!'

Poirot smiled modestly.

'No, no. Japp deserves as much credit as I do. He has

220

done wonders in identifying Gale as Richards. The Canadian police want Richards. A girl he was mixed up with there is supposed to have committed suicide, but facts have come to light which seem to point to murder.'

'Terrible,' Mr Clancy chirped.

'A killer,' said Poirot. 'And like many killers, attractive to women.'

Mr Clancy coughed.

'That poor girl, Jane Grey.'

Poirot shook his head sadly.

'Yes, as I said to her, life can be very terrible. But she has courage. She will come through.'

With an absent-minded hand he arranged a pile of picture papers that Norman Gale had disarranged in his wild spring.

Something arrested his attention – a snapshot of Venetia Kerr at a race meeting, 'talking to Lord Horbury and a friend.'

He handed it to Mr Clancy.

'You see that? In a year's time there will be an announcement: "*A marriage is arranged and will shortly take place between Lord Horbury and the Hon. Venetia Kerr.*" And do you know who will have arranged that marriage? Hercule Poirot! There is another marriage that I have arranged, too.'

'Lady Horbury and Mr Barraclough?'

'Ah, no, in that matter I take no interest.' He leaned forward. 'No – I refer to a marriage between M. Jean Dupont and Miss Jane Grey. You will see.'

It was a month later that Jane came to Poirot.

'I ought to hate you, M. Poirot.'

She looked pale and fine drawn with dark circles round her eyes.

Poirot said gently:

'Hate me a little if you will. But I think you are one of those who would rather look truth in the face than live in a

221

fool's paradise; and you might not have lived in it so very long. Getting rid of women is a vice that grows.'

'He was so terribly attractive,' said Jane.

She added:

'I shall never fall in love again.'

'Naturally,' agreed Poirot. 'That side of life is finished for you.'

Jane nodded.

'But what I must do is to have work – something interesting that I could lose myself in.'

Poirot tilted back his chair and looked at the ceiling.

'I should advise you to go to Persia with the Duponts. That is interesting work, if you like.'

'But – but – I thought that was only camouflage on your part.'

Poirot shook his head.

'On the contrary – I have become so interested in archaeology and prehistoric pottery that I sent the cheque for the donation I had promised. I heard this morning that they were expecting you to join the expedition. Can you draw at all?'

'Yes, I was rather good at drawing at school.'

'Excellent. I think you will enjoy your season.'

'Do they really want me to come?'

'They are counting on it.'

'It would be wonderful,' said Jane, 'to get right away –'

A little colour rose in her face.

'M. Poirot –' She looked at him suspiciously. 'You're not – you're not – being kind?'

'Kind?' said Poirot with a lively horror at the idea. 'I can assure you, Mademoiselle – that where money is concerned I am strictly a man of business –'

He seemed so offended that Jane quickly begged his pardon.

'I think,' she said, 'that I'd better go to some museums and look at some prehistoric pottery.'

'A very good idea.'

At the doorway Jane paused and then came back.

'You mayn't have been kind in that particular way, but you *have* been kind – to me.'

She dropped a kiss on the top of his head and went out again.

'*Ça, c'est très gentil!*' said Hercule Poirot.